The Acadian Secret

by

Tammy Lowe

The Acadian Secret

Cover Art by *Jennifer Greeff*

The Wild Rose Press, Inc.
PO Box 708
Adams Basin, NY 14410-0708
Visit us at www.thewildrosepress.com

Publishing History
First Edition, 2022
Trade Paperback ISBN 978-1-5092-4310-5
Digital ISBN 978-1-5092-4311-2

Published in the United States of America

In the late afternoon sunshine, the man's shoulders curled over his chest as he walked the familiar tree-lined street. The avenue bloomed in a profusion of spring blossoms. With a lump in his throat, he realized it hadn't changed much in appearance over time.

Kind of like him.

Instead of horses and buggies, cars now drove past. Flowers overflowing from window boxes still decorated the colorful houses and shops, chimes still rang over doorways, and people still chatted as they strolled along the main road.

When Elisabeth and her mother stepped out of the pizzeria and stopped in front of the tiny antique shop, the man's blue eyes clouded with tears. His brows pulled in as Elisabeth pointed to an object on display in the window before dragging her mother inside. A few minutes later they walked back out.

The man's chest hitched. *What have I done? Dear God, what have I done?*

He knew what the package tucked under her arm contained. A crystal timepiece, disguised as a simple necklace.

He wanted to scream, but he was a shell, empty inside except for the pain. This was the price to be paid. He must live, but live in hell, condemned to the prison of his own making until the day everything could be made right again.

Dedication

For Quinton

Always

Chapter One

Beneath the pale moonlight, two silhouettes lingered in the town's gazebo, waiting for the sun to rise. Today was the day it all began. Again. The woman ran her fingers along peeling white paint while staring across Mahone Bay. She breathed in the sea air, listening to gentle waves lap against the rocky shoreline. "Tell me what *really* happened on Oak Island."

The man flashed a mischievous grin. "If I recall correctly, you're the one who first told *me* what happened. After we fell into that mineshaft."

She turned, shooting him a bemused smile. "I only know what I've read in the history books, but *you* were there." She pulled the wide lapels of her beige trench coat together to stay warm.

"True. True." With a deep, satisfied breath, the man sat on the bench, patting the space next to him. "All right, *cor meum*, I shall tell you the tale of John Smith." He leaned forward. "Again."

Without a moment of hesitation, she shuffled closer, taking a seat beside him.

"John Smith hadn't seen a pirate ship in seven years, but..." He closed his eyes, recalling events from a long age ago. "They'd sailed to this cove for over a century. Everyone from Newfoundland to Virginia was aware Captain Kidd might have buried his stash around here somewhere. It was 1795, and settlers in Mahone Bay were busy folks of course, but while they tended to their chores, it was normal to keep an eye open for something out of place." He paused to give the woman a playful nudge. "For something that might indicate an X marked the spot."

****

"If there's pirate booty buried there, we split it three ways," John said. A huge grin spread across his face. "Deal?"

Wide-eyed, Anthony Vaughan nodded while grabbing the oars.

Danny McGinnis pointed to tiny Oak Island that lay ahead of them. "Row toward that beach."

The island was one of hundreds that dotted the bay, but the only one with oak trees growing on it. The Micmac tribe whispered to folks in town the island was haunted, but these three teens weren't afraid of ghosts. They grabbed their shovels and pickaxes and jumped out of the rowboat as soon as they were ashore.

"This way," Danny shouted. With a throaty laugh, he led the way through the woods, his lanky body easily twisting through the underbrush. "This is the way I went yesterday."

John and Anthony followed their younger friend along an old trail. When they stopped beneath a tree, Danny pointed up at a huge branch that stretched out over them. It was about sixteen feet high, but the end had been sawed off.

"Do you see that?" he asked, bouncing from foot to foot. "It's an old tackle block, the kind you use as a pulley to lift heavy stuff. And look here at the ground."

They stood in a large depression, as if someone had long ago dug a hole and then filled it up again.

"Whoa…" John said with a slow shake of his head.

The young men started digging right away. Visions of gold, silver, and priceless gemstones made the work seem light as shovels full of dirt flew over their strong shoulders.

"Bloody Helen," Anthony shouted after a short while. "I've hit something!"

John whooped. "Men, I do believe we've just found buried treasure."

With much shouting and hollering, the boys threw their shovels down and cleared the rest of the dirt away by hand. They'd unearthed a circle of flagstones. Working as fast as they could, they pried them out and tossed them aside.

"Will you look at this…we're digging up a shaft or something. Do you see that?" Anthony's voice filled with wonder, running his hands along the markings that covered the clay sides of the hole. "These are from a pickaxe. There's definitely got to be something down here."

They spent the rest of the afternoon digging. When their hole was about five feet deep and their heads were above the top, they decided to call it quits for the night. The excavation would continue in the morning.

John arranged the shovels in a neat pile and headed back to the beach with his friends. None of them said much as they rowed toward the mainland. They were exhausted and lost in thoughts of fame and fortune. The waves rocked the boat as the salty air enveloped them.

"See you in the morning. We'll meet at dawn," John said, standing outside his tiny log house.

"John Smith, supper was over an hour ago!" his mother hollered.

"I gotta go," he said. "See you tomorrow?"

Anthony nodded. "Yup, see you later."

That evening, John waited for his three little brothers to fall asleep. It seemed to take forever. The four dark-haired young men shared the same hay-filled mattress in a tiny loft. Sleep wouldn't come, of course. John's heart raced as he wondered who built the mysterious pit, and what on earth they'd buried.

Chapter Two

It didn't matter that it was a perfect spring day. The kind where the sky is so blue, the grass so green, even teachers will do just about anything not to have to spend it indoors. With an empty feeling in the pit of her stomach, twelve-year-old Elisabeth London couldn't stop biting her fingernails. Gym class was held outside last period. She hated gym. Actually, hate wasn't a strong enough word. Elisabeth loathed it, but told herself if she was going to be terrible at a school subject, it might as well be sports.

By no means would anyone call her a tomboy. Elisabeth was named after Empress Elisabeth, a beautiful Bavarian princess who once lived in the palace where her parents first met. Mom worked there as an English tour guide and Dad ended up in one of her groups.

"I was more interested in your mother than the palace," he liked to tease.

With Elisabeth's long brown hair and big brown eyes, she suited her name, and who expected such a fine young lady to be good at baseball anyhow?

She rubbed the back of her neck while stepping up to home plate. Hands trembled as memories of that September game washed over her. She hadn't anticipated any problems while in the outfield because most of the action happened at the bases. Of course, that's when a fly ball came right at her.

Everyone was yelling.

"Get it, Elisabeth!"

"Get it!"

With a booming laugh, she held the glove up over her head, watching as the ball traveled on a perfect course for her hand. "I've got it!"

Elisabeth got it all right.

She missed the ball with her glove, caught it with her eye, and had to be rushed to the hospital, screaming in agony.

The young lady sported a grotesque shiner until Halloween.

Needless to say, Elisabeth now dreaded baseball. Plus, her gym teacher made up a dumb rule that you could try as many times as necessary to hit the ball. You couldn't strike out. This wasn't a problem for anyone else, of course.

"Okay, just relax and keep your eye on the ball. You can do it," Mr. Keddy said.

Elisabeth's mouth fell open.

The man's ears turned red. "I, uh…I meant—"

"Yeah! Keep your *eye* on the ball!" Will cackled from across the field.

Elisabeth ignored Will's teasing and held up the baseball bat. Her heart pounded as she gritted her teeth and swung.

She missed and cursed under her breath. The pitcher kept pitching, but Elisabeth kept missing. Five times, six times, no matter how hard she tried, she couldn't hit the ball.

Her cheeks burned, knowing the game was at a

standstill because of her.

"It's okay, Elisabeth," her teacher said in a soothing tone while clapping. "You can do it."

Her hands trembled as everyone stared.

Again she swung.

Again, she missed.

"Strike fifteen," Will announced.

Her chest hitched. She wanted to dig a hole, right there in the middle of the field, and crawl into it.

"Strike sixteen."

Why couldn't Mr. Keddy change his dumb rule and end her humiliation?

"Strike seventeen! I think this is a new world record."

"That's quite enough, William," the teacher said through gritted teeth.

"Pretend it's Will's head you're trying to hit," someone yelled out.

As the ball edged closer, she watched, imagining Will's face coming straight at her.

Finally, she hit it, gasping in surprise when the bat made contact with the baseball. Elisabeth didn't hit a home run or anything, but from the amount of cheering that took place, you'd have never known. The game could now continue. Eighteenth time was the charm.

****

Later on, she stepped off the school bus, fighting her way through the crowded street. Elisabeth pulled in a deep breath, waiting for the tourists taking photos of her house to finish before heading to the front door. She was used to it. People always stopped to admire her historic, blue Georgian home with the white gingerbread trim.

"Betty, it looks just like a dollhouse," she overheard an old woman say to another.

Living in Mahone Bay, Nova Scotia, was kind of like living in a volcano. Every spring, the seaside town erupted and burst to life. The happy noise of festivals and concerts filled the air; yachts and classic boats sailed through the harbor, while a kilted bagpiper greeted the tourists who flocked here. The main street became congested with traffic as people stopped to snap pictures of the three old churches that stood united along the water's edge.

Once autumn came and the Great Scarecrow Festival ended, the tourists left, the yachters sailed home, and the town became dormant. Even the church bells seemed to ring a lonely lullaby. Quiet and empty, it slept until the following spring.

"I'm hungry," Elisabeth hollered as she burst through the front door, dropped her backpack on the floor, and headed toward the kitchen. "School *sucked* today. Why do they make me play baseball?"

"Hey…" Mom turned around, frowning while holding a cookie sheet in her hand. "Watch your language, young lady."

"What? Sucked?"

"Elisabeth—"

"Sorry, I just wish I could skip gym class." She slumped into a kitchen chair. "It's humiliating."

Mom let out a heavy sigh. "Sorry you had a bad day. These will cheer you up." She set a plate of chocolate chip cookies on the table. "They're still warm."

A slow smile built as Elisabeth reached for one. "At least it's Friday. Pizza and movie night."

"It'll just be the two of us this evening. Your father called earlier. One of his patients went into labour."

Elisabeth groaned. "Well, I hope she plops the baby out fast so Dad can get home."

Her mother's lips pinched together, keeping laughter at bay as she grabbed a sweater. "Come on, you nut, want to pick up the pizza with me?"

****

In the late afternoon sunshine, the man's shoulders curled over his chest as he walked the familiar tree-lined street. The avenue bloomed in a profusion of spring blossoms. With a lump in his throat, he realized it hadn't changed much in appearance over time.

Kind of like him.

Instead of horses and buggies, cars now drove past. Flowers overflowing from window boxes still decorated the colorful houses and shops, chimes still rang over doorways, and people still chatted as they strolled along the main road.

When Elisabeth and her mother stepped out of the pizzeria and stopped in front of the tiny antique shop, the man's blue eyes clouded with tears. His brows pulled in as Elisabeth pointed to an object on display in the window before dragging her mother inside. A few minutes later they walked back out.

The man's chest hitched. *What have I done? Dear God, what have I done?*

He knew what the package tucked under her arm contained. A crystal timepiece, disguised as a simple necklace.

He wanted to scream, but he was a shell, empty inside except for the pain. This was the price to be paid. He must live, but live in hell, condemned to the prison of his own making until the day everything could be made right again.

They say quartz crystal keeps the most accurate time, but Elisabeth had no idea the amount of power hers was capable of, the science behind it, nor the millennia of earth's magic within it. Why don't people believe in magic anymore? Elisabeth used to think that way, but learned the hard way it's all around us.

"Just look at nature," he had said to her that summer evening in Italy when they were both seventeen. "Does the caterpillar not turn into a majestic butterfly? Do grapes not turn into intoxicating wine, and then into vinegar?"

The man's eyes prickled with tears as Shakespeare's line drifted through his mind, reminding him instantly of something his adoptive father would have said to them. *"There are more things in heaven and earth, Horatio, than are dreamt of in your philosophy."*

The latest discovery of time crystals was a good example. Not even hypothesized until 2012, nine years later, Google's quantum computers created the first ones, completely contradicting Sir Isaac Newton's first law of motion.

The man held his breath when Elisabeth looked up at him as she walked by with her mother. Her head flinched back slightly, and he swore there was a spark of recognition in her eyes.

Impossible.

She didn't know him yet.

She wouldn't for years.

He brought a shaky hand to his forehead and reminded himself to breathe again.

****

"Ready to start the movie?"

"Yep. Just give me five minutes." Elisabeth went up to her room, changing into a comfy fuchsia nightgown. She touched her throat, twirling the new necklace absentmindedly in her fingers. It was a simple piece of jewelry, a crystal pendant about the size of a strawberry, hanging from a thin silver chain. From the shop window, it seemed to be calling to her. Even mother agreed it suited her.

Elisabeth curled up on the sofa, watching a feel-good movie. After dozing off, she was awakened by her dad carrying her upstairs. His dark hair was disheveled and his glasses were falling off the end of his nose.

"You're home," she said, yawning. "You missed a good movie. A true story about a little dog named Bobby…in Scotland."

"Ahh, Greyfriar's Bobby." He tucked her in bed, placing a gentle kiss on her forehead. "Shhh. You can tell me all about it in the morning." He straightened his glasses. "Nighty-night, princess."

She took a slow, easy breath. While thinking about her day, she twirled the necklace's crystal in her fingers and drifted back to sleep. Unknown to her, the energy within the crystal was permanently in a special form of perpetual motion.

It was about to change her life.

Forever.

Chapter Three

As the evening sun wandered behind the mountains, it cast an emerald glow across a glen. The valley was dotted with boulders, rocks, and drifts of bright yellow flowering bushes that blanketed the rolling hills, perfuming the air with a coconut scent. A small river twisted its way toward a distant forest. Overhead, a hawk screeched while soaring across an endless blue sky, declaring its vast territory to other hawks.

A dog yelped, over and over and over again.

Awakened by the barking, Elisabeth's eyes narrowed in confusion. Her chest tightened as she sat up. "What the—?"

A huge, hairy boar, with razor-sharp tusks, lunged into the nearby brambles.

With a gasp, Elisabeth scrambled behind a large rock. Her breath hitched as her mind raced to make sense of the surrounding scenery.

That's when a hunter, with a short beard and wild black hair that gave him a crazed look, came galloping over the crest of a hill on horseback. "Good boy, Talbot," he yelled when the dog lunged into the brambles after the wild pig. The angry grunts of the boar filtered through the thick shrub.

Elisabeth leaped back, ducking low to hide behind

the boulder. One hand pressed tight across her mouth.

The clip-clop stomping of the horse's hooves sounded closer. Then, the hunter's voice rose in pitch as his piercing blue-green eyes stared down at her, crouched in the heather. "What the devil...?"

A cold chill ran up her spine when he dismounted. His head cocked slightly to the side, and she realized his hearing focused on the dog and the boar as he drew closer.

Bending to peer at her, the hunter scratched his cheek. "You all right, lass?"

Elisabeth's muscles tightened and she drew her head back sharply. "Yep. Fine."

"Then...what are ye doing out here?" he asked in an uncertain tone while helping her to her feet. "Dressed in naught but...that?"

Elisabeth's mouth opened, but nothing came out.

"Well, you're lucky I found you before—" The silence in the valley now broken, Talbot howled, the boar squealed, and Elisabeth backed away with quick, jerky steps.

"Dinnae move, lass," he ordered in a steady, low-pitched voice while reaching for his dagger.

Elisabeth gasped for air, watching the enraged boar desert its hiding spot in the brambles and charge toward the dog, its lethal tusks ready to kill.

Talbot seemed well-trained so, instead of turning tail and running, he danced backward, facing the pig, luring it away from his master. With the boar now in pursuit of the dog, the hunter ran at the beast as if he were a wild animal himself. Jumping on the boar from behind, he grabbed its ear, yanked its head up, and slashed its throat.

Elisabeth's heart pounded, and she gripped the sides of her head.

The hunter jumped off the boar as it fell limp at his feet and cleaned the blade on the carcass before putting it away. He then walked toward Elisabeth, his bloody hands held in front of him.

"You've got a knife." Elisabeth whimpered as her gaze darted from the enormous man dressed in a skirt to the ragtag group of hunters who came cantering over the crest of the hill.

"Aye, and a sword." He smirked while pointing at it. "I'm not going to harm you, though. I'm hunting."

"Hunting what? Little girls?" Not waiting for an answer, she bolted, heading for the distant forest.

The hunter took a step back and chuckled as Elisabeth made her great escape in slow motion, hindered terribly by bare feet.

"You're completely mad!" he shouted while mounting his horse, motioning to the arriving men to deal with the boar carcass.

The black warhorse was as large and intimidating as the hunter and the animal's powerful legs kicked up tall grass and thistles as it galloped along. The sound of its hooves seemed amplified as it neared Elisabeth.

Without needing to slow his horse, he reached down, scooped Elisabeth into his arms, and placed her in the saddle in front of him. She let out a sharp scream.

"There. Now be a good lass. I promise I'm not going to hurt you. You're on my land so I know you're not from these parts. I cannot leave you alone out here. It's not safe and will soon be dark."

A wave of coldness caused Elisabeth to tremble. She had no idea where she was and no recollection of arriving. When the hunter wrapped her in his plaid and nudged his horse on, Elisabeth's shoulders tightened. She remained silent, bringing a shaky hand to her forehead while trying to figure out what the heck was going on. This definitely wasn't Mahone Bay anymore.

In the fading light, they eventually reached a long, winding road, and the hunter began whistling a merry tune. A lane formed beneath a dark canopy of ancient trees, their branches so long they touched the ground before growing back up again.

When they rounded a corner, Elisabeth spotted a small castle before them. Rather than being an enormous medieval fortress surrounded by thick walls, this was a single stone tower with an attached mansion house. The horse trotted out of the forest canopy and into an open courtyard.

"Shona," the hunter called to a woman up front. "Summon Lady McQuade at once."

"Aye, sir." Shona curtseyed before turning on her heel and running off, disappearing down a staircase hidden behind a stone pony wall to the right of the front door. Elisabeth guessed it was a servant's entrance. She also took note of the woman's long dress and apron.

The hunter dismounted. "Dinnae you fret," he said, lifting Elisabeth down. "We'll send for your kin straight away."

Posture slumped in relief, she wiped her nose with the back of her hand. "Thank you."

When he handed the horse off to an older man, Elisabeth's gaze darted around, still trying to figure out where she was. She crossed and uncrossed her arms while looking at the random wildflowers growing out of the gravel, and the pile of wood chips surrounding a tree stump, obviously used for cutting. Above that, a shutter creaked shut before it was latched by someone inside.

The sun was setting, so despite her better judgment, Elisabeth cleared her throat, deciding to follow the hunter. Heavy wooden doors with iron studs sat open, pushed up against the interior stone walls of a small alcove, leading to a recessed secondary front door. Once inside, three stone steps rose to an entrance hall, which smelled of wood fire. A long corridor ran both left and right, leading to various rooms. On Elisabeth's immediate right, a half-turn staircase rose to the upper floors. Glancing up, she guessed there were about four stories in this section of the castle.

She clutched her stomach as if in pain. "You're going to send for my parents, right?" she confirmed in an uncertain tone.

"Aye," was his simple reply as he walked past the staircase, into what appeared to be a rustic dining hall; its beamed ceiling blackened by soot. At the far end, a fire crackled in a fireplace that featured an ornately carved stone mantle. Rough white-washed walls were adorned with deer heads, shiny mounted swords, and painted banners.

A woman, with the same blue-green eyes as the hunter's, jerked her head back when she saw Elisabeth, who was still barefoot and dressed in a hot pink nightgown. The woman had perfect posture, a stern face with straight lips that didn't appear to smile often, and greying dark hair pulled up into a thick bun.

Elisabeth looked away to gather her thoughts. Like Shona outside, this lady also wore a long, old-fashioned dress.

"Malcolm…?" The woman's brows squished together as she marched closer. "What on earth?"

"Stay calm. She's fine, sister, absolutely fine. She is a healthy lass, and—"

"In that case, do cover yourself up, child." With a sharp tone, the woman pulled the shawl off her own shoulders to wrap around Elisabeth. "Dear God, what are you wearing? It's naught more than a nightshirt." Her nose wrinkled. "And an odd one at that." She turned to her brother, looking for answers.

"She was lost and alone in the middle of the glen." His eyes bulged. "Luckily, I found her before the boar I was hunting did. See that the bairn is tended to and locate her kin," Malcolm ordered before exiting the room.

"Umm…" Elisabeth bit her lip. "Can I just use your phone to call my parents? I need to tell them where I am so they can come get me."

The woman's eyes narrowed as she shuffled closer. "Judging by yer *tongue*, I'm going to guess you're not from around here, are ye, lass? But aye, we'll send a messenger to call for them first thing in the mornin'."

Elisabeth swallowed hard. *First thing in the morning?* Despite begging, her parents didn't think she needed a cell phone at twelve years old. Boy, were they going to be sorry. She felt mentally numb while glancing around the dimly lit room. "Where am I?"

"At Castle Ealasaid child, and lucky, too. If the laird rescued you from a wild boar, I'd say the good Lord was watching over you. We still have them in these parts, you know. Those creatures can attack a grown man something fierce."

Elisabeth rubbed her forehead. *The horses, the old-*

fashioned clothing. These people clearly had no telephone, or electricity, judging by the look of things.

Suddenly realizing where she most likely was, Elisabeth held still in expectation.

Most live on farms, but maybe rich ones live in— "So, you're…like…some type of Mennonite or Amish family, aren't you?"

"Of what clan are they?" the woman's posture perked up. "We're Scottish, seeing as you're in Scotland."

"Scotland?" Elisabeth's voice rose in pitch. "What do you mean I'm in Scotland?"

"Aye, you're in Scotland, lass. Where'd you think you were?"

Elisabeth waved the old woman off. Clearly, none of this was real. She had to be sleeping. This had to be some crazy, vivid dream.

But if she *knew* she was sleeping, why wasn't she waking up?

"What is your name, child?"

"Elisabeth. Elisabeth London."

The lady's mouth snapped shut. She then looked down, as if trying to hide her expression. "So, Elisabeth from London—"

"No, I'm from Mahone Bay."

The woman's head flinched back in confusion.

"I'm Elisabeth London from Mahone Bay, not from London," she repeated. "Can someone please call my parents?"

"Aye, child, but you'll have to spend the night here," she said while motioning to a servant. "Shona, show our guest to a room."

"Aye, ma'am."

"And Shona…"

"M'lady?"

"Bring a hot toddy to calm her nerves and help her sleep."

"Aye, ma'am."

She cocked her head. "Bring me one too."

****

"Caw. Caw."

It was a little louder, this time with laughing.

"CAW. CAW."

It wasn't a crow.

John opened his eyes and heard his friends outside. The sun was beginning to rise; it was a new day. With a light-hearted feeling, he stumbled outside in his long underwear, yawning and stretching. "I'm coming. Just give me a minute to get dressed."

"Hurry up," thirteen-year-old Danny said while bouncing from foot to foot. "We have pirate booty to dig up!"

A few minutes later, they were rowing to Oak Island. The young men climbed down into the hole and started right to work.

Hour after hour passed until it was almost ten feet deep.

"Do you think we should stop?" Danny looked up at the opening of the pit, rubbing the back of his neck. "We've been at this all day and nothing. Maybe someone's already dug it up and taken whatever was here."

"Ruddy 'ell, no." Anthony brushed blond hair from his brow. "I'm still digging."

"Me, too. I'm not ready to quit yet," agreed John.

"I don't know." Danny took a deep breath. "I hope

we're not being dunderheids," he grumbled as he resumed digging.

Moments later, Anthony's shovel hit something. "I think there's wood here. I've got something."

Fresh, new anticipation flowed through their veins as they worked to see what the obstruction was.

"I can see it. It *is* wood. It must be a treasure chest." Anthony fell to his knees. "It better be full of jewels."

"That's for sure." John's eyes were wide with anticipation. "If there're gems there, I swear to find the prettiest one of all and give it to Sarah."

John Smith thought about how close they must be to finding pirate gold, and how, when he found it, he was going to ask Sarah Floyd to marry him. He was a man now, sixteen years old, and fully expected at any moment he'd be one of the three richest men in town. He'd build a huge castle, have sixteen teams of horses, and—

"I don't know what I'm going to do with my share," Anthony said, interrupting John's daydream. "I've been up all night trying to figure that out."

Once the dirt was cleared away, it revealed a floor of sorts, made of oak logs. "John, Danny, help me lift these out."

However, the planks wouldn't budge. Upon closer inspection, the young men could see they were secured to the sides of the pit, and caulked in place with putty.

"Bloody Helen, this is going to take forever." Anthony's posture slumped as he started attacking them with his pickaxe. "Look how rotten the wood is. They must have been here for a long time."

They continued to work on the logs, removing

them one at a time. The friends were disappointed to see beneath them was more dirt.

"Keep digging?" Anthony asked.

"Yes," his friends answered in unison.

After digging a few more feet, they were forced to finish for the night, as the sun descended and light became dim. Vowing to return in the morning, they packed up and left their construction site.

Chapter Four

The hot toddy given to Elisabeth to calm her nerves had worked well and she slept through the night. However, upon awakening, her stomach clenched. This was no dream. She was still here, in a sparse, tiny bedroom. No décor except a cross on the wall. The sweet, medicinal taste of the warm drink lingered in her mouth as she turned her head and saw Shona.

The plump, plain-looking woman slept in a wooden chair beside her, softly snoring. Wearing a floor-length brown dress, her chin was tucked into her large bosom; her dull brown hair pulled back in a braid.

The grogginess gone and now awake, Elisabeth sat up and cleared her throat.

Shona's head jerked back. With a sleepy look, she scurried out of the room. "Fetch Lady McQuade at once!" she hollered down the hallway before returning.

Not a moment later, Lady McQuade entered the room—the same woman from the dining hall last night. Her full skirts took up half the floor space, and in her arms she carried a tall stack of folded clothing and a pair of leather shoes.

"You've slept through the night and half the morn, child. My grandmother's toddy is still the best medicine." With a satisfied smile, she placed the garments on the bed next to Elisabeth. "You must be hungry. Shona, fetch a plate of food."

"Aye, ma'am." The woman exited the room.

"Has anyone called my parents yet?" Elisabeth closed her eyes and took a deep breath. "They're going to be worried sick." *The police are probably even searching for me by now.*

"Aye. A messenger left at dawn for London."

Elisabeth scraped a hand over her face. How hard was it to understand she was Elisabeth London...not Elisabeth *from* London? She was going to have to get out of this compound and find a phone or something herself.

Lady McQuade patted the clothing. "I brought these for you to wear since you were found in naught but"—she sucked in a quick breath, pointing to Elisabeth's nightgown—"*that.*"

"Thank you," Elisabeth said, eying the stack of clothes. "But really, I don't need more than one dress. I won't be here much longer."

Lady McQuade lifted her brows. "I'd swear the fairy-folk left you in that glen. That *is* only one dress, child."

Elisabeth felt her cheeks flush. "Oh, I—"

"Not to worry. Shona will dress you when she returns. I have other matters to attend to, but I'll check on you again soon. Do see that you eat something," she said before leaving.

Elisabeth lay on the lumpy bed. "It's fine. Everything will be fine," she muttered to the empty room.

A short time later, Shona returned with a small tray. Elisabeth licked her lips and sat up so the woman could place it on her lap.

"Don't you fret, the laird's a—" The woman's eyes widened, watching as Elisabeth devoured a bowl of porridge.

"Sorry…I'm starving," she said with a chuckle.

"Well…eat up, then. As I was sayin', the laird's an honorable man. He's the one who found you and he'll make sure to see you in your mother and da's arms again. Now that you've got a full belly, I'll help you dress, and then you run along outside for a bit of fresh air. You should go find Quinton and Fiona, seeing you're about the same age."

Elisabeth's posture perked up. Surely anybody her age here would have a phone or some electronic device. She set the tray aside and climbed out of bed.

Shona handed her what looked like a plain white nightgown. "Here, lass. Put the leine on."

The garment was knee-length with sleeves that fell below the elbows. Elisabeth turned her back to Shona for privacy, undressed, and slipped the new garment over her head.

"All right, the stay next." Shona laced an item resembling a corset around her ribs. Its job was to force her into the correct posture, rather than making her waist appear tiny.

The servant helped Elisabeth dress in all the layers; stockings and shoes, then two petticoats, the top one being white with blue stripes. Next was a brown skirt, an apron, a neckerchief and vest, and a thin brown jacket.

"An improvement to be sure. Now, let me do something with that nest on your head. You've got leaves in your hair, child. Sit."

She sat while the woman brushed her hair and tied it back using a red ribbon. With a wide grin, Elisabeth suddenly became still, looking down at the old-fashioned clothing she wore. It felt like being on a stage set in costume.

When Shona declared her ready, Elisabeth left the bedroom and ventured down the long corridor. As she descended the half-turn staircase, each landing had a window with thick draperies overlooking the front courtyard. She was sidetracked by small, mounted deer heads and old paintings on the walls. The artists were not particularly talented, causing her to clamp both lips together to stop from laughing. Her mother was a far better painter.

Once outside, Elisabeth blinked several times, blinded momentarily by the sunshine. Beside her, a chicken clucked, scratching at the ground. In the distance, a wooden swing hanging from the branch of an ancient tree swayed gently on the breeze. Elisabeth turned around to look up at the tower once again. An unknown flag flown from the tallest turret flapped in the wind. Her pulse increased. "How did I get here?" she mumbled.

As she wandered across the courtyard, people dressed in old-fashioned clothes were going about a variety of chores. A slow smile grew when Elisabeth saw Malcolm walking toward her. Head tilted to the side, she examined his attire. Like yesterday, he wore a dull plaid fabric wrapped and belted over a white tunic. The bottom half made a skirt and the top half was thrown over his shoulder and pinned in place. It was as if he had swaddled himself in a blanket. Elisabeth stopped mid-stride and did a double-take, glancing around the entire scene. For a moment, it felt like she had stepped back in time. With a nervous laugh, she turned her attention back to Malcolm as he approached.

"Ah, 'tis good to see my wee bonnie friend looking well-rested this morning." He then leaned closer. "So I must ask…what the devil were you doing in that remote glen, all by yourself, lass?"

She let out a long exhale. "I actually have no idea how I got there, sir."

Malcolm's brow furrowed. "And you're from…Mahone Bay?"

"Yes."

The laird tugged at his ear. "The thing is…no one knows this Mahone Bay you speak of."

Elisabeth's mouth fell open. How far from home was she? She couldn't *really* be in Scotland.

Malcolm pursed his lips. "For generations, our family has vowed never to turn a person in need away, especially a bairn like yourself. I do not know what to make of you, so until I do, you're to think of Castle Ealasaid as your home."

Elisabeth replied with a hesitant nod as Malcolm took his leave.

She strolled across the courtyard and then alongside a low wall made of stacked stones. The air smelled of sun-warmed earth and wildflowers. Elisabeth heard peals of laughter and shouting ahead.

Kids' voices.

With a fluttery feeling in her stomach, she followed the happy noise into the trees, along a deeply shaded footpath dotted with ferns.

Before long, the back of a girl came into view. Dressed in a burgundy skirt and brown jacket, she swung her arms while walking.

A boy with wild brown hair, dressed in an off-white shirt and brown knee-length pants, bounced on his toes behind her, gently tugging the girl's jet-black braid. "You know what I heard, Fiona?"

"No, what?"

"When you were born, your mother thought you were a treasure…"

Fiona waved her hand, brushing off the compliment.

"But you were so ugly your father said…" The boy let out a belly laugh before reaching the punchline. "Your father said, 'aye, let's bury it.'"

Elisabeth pressed a fist against her lips to stop from laughing.

With a groan, Fiona gave him a playful smack. "My ma said when you were born the midwife slapped your mother instead of you."

Elisabeth couldn't help giggling.

Fiona gasped, turned around, and then let out a bark of laughter. "We didn't know anyone was there." She had green eyes, and a big smudge of dirt across her nose. "Who are you?"

The boy's hazel eyes widened. "You must be Elisabeth." He took a step back and turned to Fiona. "She's a lass my Uncle Malcolm found. Everyone says she's run off from some village nobody's heard of and—"

Elisabeth winced. "You've never heard of Mahone Bay?"

He shook his head. "Aye, they're right. You do ''ave an accent nobody recognizes." The boy then shrugged his shoulders. "I'm Quinton McQuade and

27

this ugly, pathetic little creature is Fiona McAllister. Now…I insist you tell me what—"

"Oh, just ignore him." With a giggle, Fiona leaned in closer to Elisabeth. "He expects everyone to do what he tells them and acts like he's laird of this land." She then gave Quinton a good-natured shove before bouncing off.

With a wide grin, he chased after her.

Fiona turned around, waving her arm. "Come on, Elisabeth!"

And with that, Elisabeth ran after them. She could hear water trickling around rocks and smelled rotting bark and leaves.

Quinton and Fiona waited for her to catch up, leading the way over uneven ground to a creek.

A frog croaked as Fiona hopped across wet stones to the other side of the tiny stream. "Quinton, you be the goat. Elisabeth, do you know how to play clench-a-wench?"

"Clench-a-wench?" She let out a hearty laugh while shaking her head. "No. I've never heard of it before."

"It's easy. We'll teach you," said Fiona.

They kept Elisabeth entertained with their game of tag, shrieking with laughter and splashing in the water. For a while, all thoughts of where she was, and how she was going to get back home, disappeared.

"I have to go now, you ken," Quinton said with a heavy sigh.

Elisabeth bit her lip. "Before you go, does one of you have a phone I could borrow?"

Both their postures perked up.

Fiona edged closer. "What's that? Have you got

one, Quinton?"

"Aye, probably," he said, feigning boredom. "I've probably got lots of them."

Elisabeth let out a huge breath. "Oh, thank God."

Fiona's eyebrows rose. "What are they?"

"They're..." Quinton clasped his hands together. "No idea," he finally confessed with a half-hearted shrug before breaking into a run. "I have to go."

Elisabeth let out a theatrical groan.

"Quinton, wait! Elisabeth and I will walk with you," Fiona called out as she tried to catch up to him. "Wait for us."

"Hurry up, then," he said, tapping his foot lightly. "I'm already late."

"Shouldn't you be at your lessons, lad?" Malcolm asked as the three children dashed by him in the courtyard.

"Aye, Uncle. I'm on my way anon." He then waved to Fiona and Elisabeth before racing inside.

Fiona quickly smoothed down her dress and turned around. "Good day to you, Laird Craig."

Elisabeth glanced at Fiona. Her eyes were bright and glossy as one hand fluttered in a dainty, feminine fashion while batting long eyelashes. However, the fact her hair was so messy and dress so dirty made the entire effect rather comical.

With a smile, Malcolm turned around and walked back toward the girls.

"This is my dear friend, Elisabeth." Fiona had a silly grin on her face. "Elisabeth, may I introduce you to Laird Craig."

"Good morning, lass. To what do I owe this pleasure?" With a bemused smile, he kissed her hand while Fiona giggled.

"Oh no, the pleasure is all mine, sir," Elisabeth said with an awkward curtsey.

"Well, it is truly an honour to meet you." He winked at Elisabeth and made a dramatic bow before leaving.

Fiona let out an appreciative sigh and watched him as he walked away. Once out of sight, she turned to Elisabeth, linking their arms together. "It's just the two of us now."

Elisabeth strolled alongside her new friend, heading straight for the tree with the wooden swing. Not knowing what to say, she said the first thing that popped into her head. "I'm twelve, but I'll be thirteen in a couple of weeks. How old are you?"

"I don't know, exactly. I'm probably the same." She let go of Elisabeth's arm and took a seat on the swing. Grabbing the rope in both hands, Fiona pushed off and started pumping her legs. "I know I was born sometime in the spring."

Elisabeth snorted in amusement as she sat on the grass, leaning against the enormous tree trunk. "What do you mean 'sometime in the spring'? Don't you know the date? What year were you born?"

"I don't know for sure," Fiona answered while swinging back and forth. "I think 1642. Why?"

Elisabeth's eyes widened. "What do you mean 1642?" She stared at Fiona, heart pounding. "Are you serious?"

"Aye." Fiona's brows squished together as she swung higher and higher. "Why? What's the matter?"

Elisabeth covered her ears. "Fiona, it's not the 1600s. This can't *possibly* be the 1600s."

Fiona burst into laughter, but then stopped pumping her legs, jumping off the swing once realizing Elisabeth wasn't joking. "You're serious, aren't you?"

Elisabeth's chest hitched as her mind raced. The strange castle, the weird clothing…it all made sense in a strange sort of way. But the 1600s? How could this happen? People can't travel back through time.

Or can they?

As she stared up at Fiona, an involuntary tremble shook her. "Do you know what a car is? A TV? An airplane? A microwave oven? Do you even know what electricity is?"

With a blank look on her face, Fiona flopped down beside her, shaking her head.

Elisabeth let out an uncontrollable whimper. "Are you telling me…this is the seventeenth century?"

Fiona's fingers reached up to touch her parted lips. "What century are you from?" she whispered.

"The twenty-first," Elisabeth said, bringing a shaky hand to her forehead.

****

John was up, waiting for his friends the next morning.

By the time the sun was waking, they met at the shore and rowed to the tiny island.

"Did you remember the rope and bucket?" Danny asked with a wide grin.

"Of course." John bit down on a smile. "Did either of you tell anyone what we're doing?"

"Nobody," said Anthony. "You?"

"Nuh-uh." Danny closed his eyes and squealed. "Three people is more than enough to be splitting pirate booty with, thank you very much!"

John leaned in. "Good, let's keep it that way. I keep telling my folks we're hunting. My father says we're mighty lousy hunters since we've yet to come home with a single thing."

Anthony laughed. "I told my parents the same thing, only I said we were fishing."

Next to their pit, young Danny easily climbed the tree onto the outstretched branch from which the old tackle block hung. With great care, he attached a new pulley system to the limb and threaded the strong rope through it.

"Looks good, McGinnis," Anthony said, while tying the bucket to the end of the rope. "Since the pit is so deep now, we'll lower ourselves in and out of the hole using the bucket as a seat. Once we're in the pit, we can use the pail to remove the dirt, one bucket at a time." He cleared his throat. "All right, lower me down...*slowly*. Bloody Helen, it better hold me."

They threw their shovels into the pit and then lowered Anthony into it. Danny raised the empty bucket back up, and John placed it behind his thighs and was lowered into the hole next.

More digging, more shaft walls. The deeper they got, the longer it took to remove the dirt. Every time they filled the bucket, Danny would hoist it up and dump it out before sending it back down again.

He stood at the edge of the hole, looking down at his friends. "How far down you think we are now?"

"I'd say it has to be over fifteen feet, don't you think?" Anthony shouted up at him.

"Oh, yeah, at least."

The afternoon wore on, and the young men became tired, achy, and hungry. When they'd dug down to the twenty-foot level, their shovels hit something.

"Bloody Helen, what's it this time?" Anthony scratched his jaw. "Do you think this is it? The treasure?"

"It's got to be." John's heart was racing. "Who'd bury anything deeper than this?"

After clearing away the dirt, Anthony let out a heavy sigh. "Another log floor." His broad shoulders slumped before he began prying the logs up and hauling them out of the pit. "Once we remove these planks, if the treasure isn't there, let's call it a day."

Having found nothing more than dirt below the logs, they left the island earlier than the previous day and headed back home. As John walked down the main street of town, he heard a familiar feminine giggle.

With an appreciative sigh, he turned and noticed Sarah in the shadows.

His Sarah, with her wild, dark brown curls.

Then, his mouth fell open as he watched her kiss Thomas Moody on the cheek.

She smoothed down her skirt, walking over when she saw him. "Hello, John."

"Don't you 'hello, John' me," he said with sweeping arm gestures. "I *just* saw you kissing Tom Moody."

Sarah looked down for a moment to hide a grin.

"Oh, John, it didn't mean anything. I was being hospitable. He was helping me with something."

"But, I thought you were my girl?"

"You never asked me." Her hands locked together.

He gave her an incredulous look. "Well, darn it, Sarah...I thought we had an understanding."

"Do you want to ask me something?"

"You're my girl, Sarah Floyd."

"Maybe. Maybe not. I didn't do anything wrong. I was just having a bit of fun."

"I don't want you to be having any more fun."

"John Smith!"

"I mean…" He shook his head. "I mean, without me."

"A girl can get lonely waiting for you to ask her anything, John Smith. You're never around anymore. What have you, Danny, and Anthony been up to, anyhow?"

"Oh, nothing. Hunting." He held his breath, imagining the gifts he was going to lavish on her as soon as he found that treasure.

"Hunting? Anthony told his father you were fishing."

"Oh, yeah, well, we were. Fishing and hunting. Manly things. You know how it is. I have to go now. I'll talk to you soon, Sarah," John said as he walked toward his house. "And remember, no more being hospitable," he shouted over his shoulder. *Especially* to Tom Moody."

The days passed and the young men continued to dig. The work may have slowed, but their excitement and enthusiasm didn't.

"Nobody would go through this much trouble if they weren't hiding something valuable."

Danny gently bit his lip. "I think it's Captain Kidd's treasure, don't you?"

"Well, I'm thinking it's definitely pirate booty," Anthony said. "This island is the perfect hiding spot. You've got the bay protecting it from the ocean, and look how well hidden Oak Island is from the

34

mainland."

Danny nodded. "Just think, out of more than three hundred islands, this is the only one with oak trees. If you hid treasure on it, the oaks would let you know straight away you had the right island."

"Now, I hate to say this…" Anthony pulled at his ear. "As much as I don't want to split the booty with anyone other than us three, I think we have to get some more men involved. We need help."

John answered with a small nod. "What about Sam?"

Samuel Ball Jr. was one of John's closest friends, so it seemed obvious they let him in on the secret, too. Samuel's father had been born a slave on a plantation in South Carolina, but after fighting with the British in the American Revolutionary war, he fled to Nova Scotia as a free man and a Loyalist. Now, at eighteen, Samuel himself was a landowner.

"Definitely Sam," Anthony said. "What about David?"

David Perrier had recently moved to the area and had become a good friend of Samuel's.

"David? He's ruddy brilliant," Danny said, wide-eyed. "He'll definitely know how to help us recover the booty."

They quit for the day and rowed their little boat back to the mainland. It was time to contact their friends.

Chapter Five

Fiona leaned closer, rubbing Elisabeth's back. "Dinnae you fret. We'll find a way to get you home. There has to be a way because you got here somehow. You'll see. It'll all work out."

Elisabeth exhaled, looking up, enjoying the warm sunshine caressing her face. "I hope so."

"Come on." Fiona's tone was gentle as she rose to her feet, then all the way to her tippy toes. "I know something that will lift your spirits."

With a strained smile, Elisabeth let Fiona take her hands and pull her up.

As they strolled through a meadow, the birds serenaded them from tree tops. Elisabeth picked a wildflower, tucking the long stem behind her ear. "I guess if I'm going to be stuck somewhere for the time being, this place isn't half bad." She let out a long exhale. "Plus, I already like you...even though we only met a few hours ago."

Fiona nodded, linking her arms through Elisabeth's again. "And I already like you too."

"You remind me of Diana Barry. Plus, she has black hair like you."

"Well, I don't know her."

Elisabeth giggled. "No, I don't suppose you do." Ever since I was little, my mom—"

Both girls froze, holding their breath when a deer stepped into view just a few yards ahead. The doe stared at them wide-eyed for a moment, as if judging whether they were a threat. Deciding they weren't, it relaxed, strolling leisurely across the meadow before disappearing into the forest.

With a slow shake of her head, Elisabeth continued. "My mom loves reading stories to me. She'll curl up on my bed and sometimes my dad even lies down, right on the floor in my room, so he can hear the story too. In the summer, we all sit on the porch and read together.

Fiona's eyes widened.

"One of my mom's favorite books is *Anne of Green Gables*. It's about an orphaned girl named Anne Shirley who is mistakenly sent to live with an elderly brother and sister—"

"That sounds just like you living here!"

"You're right," Elisabeth said with a bark of laughter. "Well, except for the orphan part. But, when Anne first came to live at Green Gables, she met a girl named Diana Barry, and right away they knew they were best friends. Kindred spirits, as Anne called them."

Fiona took a deep breath. "Kindred spirits. I like that."

Arms linked together, the girls walked alongside the courtyard. A short distance away, under a nearby tree, they could see Quinton with his school books, trying to pay attention to his tutor's lesson. Fiona mocked him with silly gestures for a few moments, while he did his best to ignore her. Afterward, they followed a dirt road away from the castle, heading toward what looked like a stone cottage.

Fiona's eyes sparkled with mischief. "Let's go ride Dandy, Quinton's horse."

"Really?" Elisabeth said with a huge grin.

"Aye, really."

The cottage turned out to be a stable; two stories tall with a wide doorway in the center and two circular windows on the upper level. A thin, old man, with a hunched back, walked out. When he saw the girls, his eyes narrowed.

Elisabeth's smile vanished.

"What might you be wantin', Fiona?" the balding man asked in a sharp tone.

"Nothing, Joseph. We're just out for a *dauner*."

He crossed his boney arms. "Don't even *think* aboot taking Master Quinton's horse." Joseph then turned, shaking his head while muttering under his breath as he walked back into the stable. The way his hands swung limply beside his skinny bow legs made him look like a character straight out of a cartoon.

Elisabeth's shoulders slumped. She'd been looking forward to riding a horse.

The girls walked around to the side of the building and Fiona stepped up onto the split rail fence, her brow furrowed as she looked at the horses grazing in the paddock. "Dandy must be inside," she said with a curt nod. "When Joseph isn't looking, I'll—"

Elisabeth gasped and stepped up onto the wooden fence beside her. "You're not going to steal the horse, are—?"

"Trust me," Fiona said with a booming laugh. "We just need to wait for the right moment to *borrow* Dandy." She suddenly glanced beyond Elisabeth and squealed with delight.

Elisabeth turned to see what her friend was looking at, chuckling when she saw Malcolm, trailed by Talbot, marching down the driveway toward the stables.

With a beaming face, Fiona jumped down from the fence, half skipping toward him.

"Oh, wee Fiona, I recognize that mischievous smile of yours. You look like you are up to no good." Malcolm exchanged a knowing look with her and then held up a hand. "Wait, I don't even want to know. Shouldn't you be off spinning or mending, like a good, proper lass?"

She brushed hair away from her face. "Laird Craig, I'm always behaving myself. The things I get in trouble for are only half of the things I think of doing, you know."

"Aye, I *do* know." For a moment, his gaze drifted over to Elisabeth, still standing on the fence rail. "You two seem to be getting along quite well."

"We're kindred spirits," Fiona said with an easy nod.

Malcolm's eyes widened. "Well…I'm glad to hear it." He shook his head, chuckling as he walked to the stable and through the doorway, with Talbot following at his heel.

Fiona ran back, grabbed Elisabeth's hand, and they crept around to the entrance where Malcolm had disappeared. They both edged closer, trying to see and hear.

"Joseph, I need my horse to be ready within the hour."

"Aye, sir." The old man's voice softened. "Have you any news from Dunnottar, sir?"

Malcolm drew in a slow, steady breath. "Aye, and none of it good."

"Has…" Joseph scrubbed a hand over his face. "Has the situation changed?"

"Not yet. The garrison is still holding, but Cromwell is on his way with more of his army."

"Oh, saints above." His tone deepened. "He's determined to find and destroy them, isn't he, sir?"

"Aye, he is. He wants nothing more than to be responsible for their destruction."

"God willing, sir, he shall not succeed."

"The siege is nearing its fifth month. I dinnae ken how much longer they can last and now with more men on the way…" Malcolm looked down. "Well, there is a plan in the making, Joseph. Pray it works."

"Oh, I will pray, sir. He's a very evil man."

"Aye, that he is. He'll stop at nothing."

A moment later, Malcolm walked out of the stable with a fast-paced stride, preoccupied to the point of not noticing the two girls still standing beside the doors.

"Come, Talbot," he called to his dog.

Fiona stroked her neck as she watched him walk away. "I'm going to marry him when I'm older. Is he not the most wonderful and handsome man who ever lived?"

Elisabeth's head jerked back and she burst into laughter. "Fiona, you are one love-sick puppy."

Fiona squinted in amusement. "Love-sick puppy? I guess I do follow him around like Talbot." She then bounced on her toes while turning, pointing across the meadow to the edge of the forest. "Do you see that grove of trees?"

Elisabeth's pulse raced. "Yes…?"

"Run over there as fast as you can. I'll join you anon."

"What?"

Fiona gave her a shove while giggling. "Go!"

Elisabeth ran across the field of wildflowers to where they'd earlier seen the deer, near the edge of the forest. Waiting beneath yet another enormous tree, she raked a hand through her hair, watching for Fiona.

After a few minutes, she paced back and forth.

The tall grasses swished in the wind.

Elisabeth eventually took a seat on an old tree stump. With a heavy sigh, she rested her chin in her hand. It probably hadn't worked. Fiona was most likely caught by Joseph and was now—

At that moment, a beautiful chestnut horse, with a young girl atop, came into view. As they galloped closer, Elisabeth could see Fiona's beaming face with an enormous smile. She leaned forward in the saddle, clearly having the time of her life. When they neared Elisabeth, the horse slowed.

"Well, are you going to get on?" Fiona asked, a gleam in her eye after bringing Dandy to a stop.

Elisabeth bit her lip while staring up at the saddle, then at the stirrup, not sure what to do. She felt her ears turning red. "I've never ridden a horse before."

"Really? You've *never* ridden a horse before?"

"Never...well, except for when Malcolm kidnapped me."

Fiona gasped. "What?"

"Well, I thought he was kidnapping me. Turns out, I'm a dork, and he was actually saving my life."

"Oh, you are so, so lucky," she said with a slow, disbelieving shake of her head. "I'd give anything to be rescued by the laird. You have to tell me *everything* that happened."

Elisabeth leaned in, stroking Dandy's side. "I have no idea how I ended up in the middle of nowhere, but Malcolm was hunting a huge, wild boar when he discovered me. You should have seen the tusks on this thing. And the smell…"

Fiona's eyes widened.

"I didn't know who Malcolm was, but…" Elisabeth waved her arms in the air with grand gestures. "He had a knife…and a sword. After he killed the boar, I tried to escape. But…he rode back to me, lifted me onto his horse in one swift move, and carried me off to his castle."

"Elisabeth…" Fiona suddenly became still. "You are, without a doubt, the luckiest girl in the entire world."

"And that's the only time I've been on a horse," she said with a belly laugh.

Fiona's shoulders pushed back while looking around. She then pointed to the tree stump. "Go stand on that."

Elisabeth obeyed and Fiona brought Dandy over, lining him up with the stump. At this height, she was now able to mount the horse with ease.

"Hang on," Fiona called as they cantered through the meadow.

Elisabeth clutched Fiona's dress, her heartbeat racing with excitement and apprehension.

When they entered the woods, Dandy slowed to a trot, following the path for a short time. Before long, they came to a clearing and upon a small stone cottage with a thatched roof and three shuttered windows. Long grasses grew against the walls. Beside the front door was a rustic bench, a bucket placed atop it. A lone chicken broke away from a small flock, racing toward the girls like a pet dog would.

Fiona dismounted near a wood pile and tied the horse to a fence post beside a water trough. She helped Elisabeth down, and then with a satisfied sigh, scooped the excited chicken into her arms, stroking its head. "This is Bonnie." She planted a kiss on the hen's head. "I won't let mother cook you," she whispered to it.

Elisabeth glanced around the property, noticing an abandoned bird's nest under the eaves. To her left, a garden was filled with neat rows of vegetables. Beside that was a huge barrel used to collect rainwater.

A theatrical groan caught her attention.

"Out! Out! Out!"

A woman appeared in the doorway, shooing a mooing cow out of the cottage before she stepped back inside, oblivious to the girls.

Elisabeth's mouth fell open. She pressed a fist against her lips to keep from laughing.

Fiona shook her head, trying not to giggle. "That cow *loves* my mother," she said. "Drives mother mad though."

"Fee!" A young girl ran toward her, followed by an even smaller boy.

"Ellen! Ian! I haven't seen you in so long…since at least this morning." With a slow, easy breath, Fiona put Bonnie, the chicken, down.

"Mama is cross with you, Fee." Ellen twisted her hair. "She says you have no sense at all."

"Uh-oh," Fiona mumbled, giving her little sister a playful pinch.

The children scampered off. Ian chasing after the chickens, while Ellen lured the cow away from the house.

Fiona walked to the bucket atop the bench by the door, taking a big drink of water from a ladle kept in it. "Have some," she said, wiping her mouth with the back of her hand.

"Thanks." Elisabeth gulped down some water, not realizing how thirsty she'd become. Her throat now quenched, she followed Fiona through the door.

Rubbing the back of her neck, Mrs. McAllistair looked up from a pot she was stirring. Elisabeth's posture perked up as her gaze darted around the tiny home. It had dirt floors and a table with wooden chairs in front of a fireplace. In one corner was a lumpy bed. Scattered throughout were a few more pieces of furniture, including a chest, a hutch holding dishes, a spinning wheel, and not much else, except for a baby lamb sleeping in the corner.

"Fiona." The woman let out a huge breath. "Where've you been, child? You know you've still got your chores to do, lass."

"Mama, please..." She clasped her hands together under her chin. "Can I play with Elisabeth some more first? She's a guest of the laird at Castle Ealasaid, and we're kindred spirits."

The woman's mouth fell open. "Kindred spirits are ye, now?" She paused, offering Elisabeth a bemused smile.

Fiona bounced on her toes. "Aye, and I promise...you can give me *ten* times as many chores tomorrow."

Mrs. McAllister clamped her lips together while

continuing to stir the contents in the pot. "Ten times as many chores?"

"Aye," Fiona said, holding still in anticipation.

Finally, her mother let out a long exhale. "All right, but be home in time for supper, lass."

With thanks, the girls hurried outside. Fiona untied Dandy, walked him over to a tree stump, using it to mount the horse with ease. Elisabeth followed suit and within moments, they were cantering away.

****

John Smith walked into Molly Malone's and spotted who he was looking for. Samuel Ball Jr. sat at a table across from his friend, David Perrier. Molly Malone's was the town's only inn. With beds upstairs, travelers were never denied a place to sleep, even though sometimes it meant sharing a bed with a stranger. Downstairs in the main room, men from the town gathered to talk about politics. Molly's was the place to go when you wanted to catch up on the latest gossip.

John held his breath as he pulled up a chair. "Hey, how would you two like a cut in some pirate booty?" he whispered.

David's ears perked up, while Samuel laughed and shook his head.

"Seriously." John leaned in. "We've discovered something huge."

He explained the details. How Danny discovered the spot, how they had spent weeks digging, and how they now needed more men and a better plan.

"I don't know." Samuel scratched his cheek. "I've a farm to run now, and soon a wife to take care of."

John's head jerked back. "A *wife*?"

"Yes. A wife," he said with a satisfied smile. "I went to Halifax last week to ask for Mary's hand. Sorry, but I don't have the time to help you dig for some treasure that mightn't even exist."

"What mightn't even exist?" Molly Malone asked while clearing away Samuel's plate.

"Smith, McInnis, and Vaughan are convinced they've found buried treasure." Samuel let out a small laugh. "They've dug down twenty-five feet already."

Molly's posture stiffened. "You dug twenty-five feet? Have you three hobbadehoys lost your marbles?"

David cleared his throat. "Where is it?"

"Oak Island."

Molly gasped. "Oak Island? Good luck getting *any* help. Everyone knows that island is cursed." With a furrowed brow, she leaned in closer and lowered her voice. "My granddad told me when he was a boy they saw mysterious lights on it. A man from town rowed a boat out there to investigate, but he was never seen again. That was seventy-five years ago and nobody's stepped foot on that island since. You be careful over there. I'd hate to see something tragic happen to you boys while you're chasing silly fantasies."

"Oh, come on Sam, David, there's something there. You should see it," John said after Molly walked away from the table.

Samuel's lips pinched together into a grimace. "Winter's coming soon. I've got a crop to harvest—"

John shook his head. "Don't say no yet. Join us in the morning. Once you see it, you'll change your mind."

"I don't know, John—"

"I'm telling you, just come and see it."

Samuel let out a dejected sigh. "Fine, but I'm not promising anything."

"What about you, David? You in?" John asked, holding still in expectation.

David's brow furrowed before he eventually nodded. "Yeah, I'm in."

The next morning, John and Anthony were deep inside their pit. They had dug to the thirty-foot mark and were in the process of removing a third oak platform.

"Hey!" a voice shouted down.

"That's got to be Sam. I knew he'd come," John said to Anthony before hollering up to him, "Hey, Samuel. Can you—?"

"You boys have exactly thirty seconds to get yourselves out of there," a voice roared down at them.

It wasn't Samuel.

John's hands went limp and Anthony swallowed hard as he looked up. "Bloody Helen," he mumbled under his breath.

It seemed their days of treasure hunting were over.

The young men grabbed the rope and hoisted their way out of the pit, one at a time. This wasn't going to be pretty.

John's father drew in a slow, steady breath. "I am absolutely speechless." His nostrils flared. "I have no idea what to say, except to thank the good Lord you didn't get yourselves killed."

"Father, you've got to see this, though. We're onto something big here."

"I can see that, son, but I can't let you keep digging." He rolled his sleeves up. "This entire pit could cave in on you. I can't believe it hasn't already.

You boys are going to have to fill it back in and forget about it."

"But, Father—"

"No buts, John. I understand your excitement. For aught I know, I'd have done the same thing at your age, but Lord Almighty, I can't let you keep at this. You've got a death trap here waiting for something to go wrong."

"But, Mr. Smith—" Anthony began.

"No. We're not discussing this any further. Grab a shovel."

John scowled as he began to throw the dirt they had spent weeks removing back into the hole.

"Oh, good. You men can lend a hand," Mr. Smith said when Samuel and David arrived a few minutes later. "We're filling this back in before someone gets killed."

Samuel shrugged his shoulders. "Not the best timing on my part," he said as he, too, started shoveling.

David chuckled and grabbed a shovel as well.

John knew his father was right. Autumn was around the corner, and there was a lot to do at harvest to prepare for the winter. They would bide their time until next spring and see if they couldn't come up with another solution.

Chapter Six

The girls spent the rest of the afternoon with Dandy, eventually returning the horse to the stable after watching Joseph leave, when a bell rang out. As they strolled back into the courtyard, Shona came marching toward them, shaking her head.

"Good Lord, lassies." She crossed her arms. "I dinnae expect you to stay away for so long. The family's already in the great hall," she said to Elisabeth. "Fiona, come down to the kitchen with me. Jonnet has a hamper you can bring home to your ma. There's some biscuit bread in it."

With a wide grin, Fiona disappeared down the stairs behind the pony wall. "Bye, Elisabeth," she called out.

"See you later, Fee."

Elisabeth clutched her hands while heading to the front entrance, wondering what they'd be serving for dinner. Her stomach growled just thinking about it. Once inside, she walked up the stone steps and down the corridor toward the dining hall. Laughing voices grew louder, chairs dragged across the floor, and dishes thumped against the table.

"Hello," Elisabeth called out, rubbing the back of her neck as she entered the room. "Sorry I'm late."

Quinton gave her a friendly nod.

Lady McQuade plucked at her clothing. "I understand you've met Fiona." She looked up with a grin.

"Aye, apparently they're *kindred spirits*," Malcolm said with a wink. "Have a seat, lass." He pointed at the chair next to Quinton.

Elisabeth took a seat at the heavy table. It ran along the left-hand side of the room and could have sat more than twenty people comfortably. This lavish home was so different from Fiona's rustic cottage. Here, candles flickered from silver candelabras. Fancy goblets and porcelain dishes graced the table. It was in stark contrast to the water pail with a communal ladle and simple wooden bowls she had noticed at Fiona's house.

"Thank you," Elisabeth said with a smile as a servant placed a plate in front of her. When she looked down at it, her smile froze and she leaned back. It didn't look like anything mom made.

"And how was Mr. Rose?" Lady McQuade asked her brother.

"Fine. Fine. But he's concerned about an outbreak of rabies. Seems a mad dog killed some of his livestock."

The woman's head jerked back. "How dreadful."

Quinton's posture perked up. "Uncle Malcolm, tell Mother the story about the goat eating your plaid this afternoon."

While Malcolm had the room in hysterics as he related the tale, Elisabeth rubbed a hand against her heart. She was suddenly homesick, tired, and hungry for her own mother's cooking. This was a wonderful family, but it wasn't *her* family.

The moment dinner was over, she excused herself

and climbed the staircase to the fourth floor, passing all the portraits on the walls. She wandered along the corridor, trying to remember which door led to the little bedroom she'd spent the night in.

Soft footsteps startled her.

"Miss Elisabeth…" Shona held a candle lantern up just as Elisabeth glanced behind. "You've been moved to another room whilst you are a guest here."

Her posture perked up. "Oh. Uh…okay." She walked to where the servant stood waiting and followed her down a flight of stairs.

One floor below, off a much grander hallway, Shona came to a stop and opened a door. Elisabeth's entire face lit up. It was nothing at all like the sparse tiny closet she'd woken up in this morning. This room smelled like sunshine and fresh linen. A large canopy bed was flanked with two side tables; a vase of wildflowers atop one. The thick curtains around the bed matched the curtains hanging from a window alcove. They were tied back, highlighting the little nook beyond. An upholstered wooden bench tucked inside created the ideal window seat. Chairs were scattered here and there, several paintings decorated the walls, and a large armoire filled the rest of the space.

Elisabeth sucked in a quick breath, taking it all in. "This must be the prettiest room in the entire castle."

"Aye, well…" Shona rubbed her chin and then placed the lantern on one of the side tables. "Lady McQuade's orders. In the cupboard, you'll find some skirts and things of that nature, seeing you had none when you arrived. Is there anything else you need, lass?"

"No. Thank you. This is more than perfect."

"Well, goodnight then. See you in the morrow," Shona said before leaving the room, closing the door behind her.

With a slow, disbelieving shake of her head, Elisabeth glanced around once again, feeling like a princess. She bounced across the room to the armoire, throwing the doors wide open. Inside, along with more skirts and jackets and petticoats, was her folded fuchsia nightgown. Her eyes prickled with tears. She picked it up, buried her nose in the familiar fabric, and was instantly reminded of home. It smelled freshly laundered.

With a shallow sigh, Elisabeth changed into the nightgown before curling up on the seat in the window alcove. Her room overlooked the front of the castle. She could see the courtyard below, the swing beyond that, and the row of ancient trees that lined the front drive.

A heavy feeling crept into her chest. She'd been fighting it off all day by managing to stay busy with Quinton, and especially Fiona. However, now, all alone, her thoughts took over.

The room grew dim as twilight arrived. She'd be spending a second night in this castle. Her hands trembled, wondering if she was stuck here forever. That's when Elisabeth spotted her friend down below. As soon as she opened the window, Fiona's laughter was carried up on the breeze.

Malcolm was walking toward the front door, shouting over his shoulder. "You best be running home now, lass. It's almost dark and your Mother will be worried aboot you, though that's nae unusual." He then disappeared into the castle.

"Fiona!" Elisabeth called down in a loud whisper.

"What are you still doing here?"

Fiona moved closer, holding up a wicker basket, whispering back just as loudly. "Jonnet gave me some food to bring home to mother, so I thought it best I help her in the kitchen a while."

Elisabeth's forehead wrinkled. "Fee?"

"Aye?"

She let out a heavy sigh. "Do you think...I mean...I don't want to get you in trouble at home, but can you stay for a *few* more minutes?" She forced a watery smile into place.

Fiona replied with an understanding nod. "Aye, but you're going to have to sneak me inside first." She pointed at the front door. "The castle is locked up for the night now."

"I'll be right down."

She latched the window, crept out into the hallway, and eased her bedroom door closed while peering around.

An eerie quiet filled the corridor.

Candle-lit lanterns flickered on the walls.

As she tiptoed along, the soft glow from a crackling fire spilled out from a common room. From the open doorway, she saw Shona, deep in conversation while tending to Lady McQuade. Elisabeth stood in the shadows, watching. When they looked away, she slunk past, shuffling along the corridor and then dashing down the staircase.

Oh crap!

Heartbeat racing, Elisabeth slid behind a thick curtain on the first landing as a maid walked up the stairs. She held her breath until the woman was gone before continuing down to the locked main doors. The first one unlatched easily, but the second had a heavy wooden bar across it. She gritted her teeth, straining while lifting the bar to push it open a crack. Fiona was there, waiting, and managed to enter the castle. Together, they replaced the bar and tiptoed upstairs.

With a fluttery feeling in her stomach, Elisabeth led the way back along the shadowy hallway. She stopped outside of the common room and glanced behind at Fiona, a finger to her lips.

They peeked inside.

It was empty.

Elisabeth's pulse increased and she glanced around, not knowing where the women had gone. "Follow me," she whispered.

They continued tiptoeing down the hall, eventually arriving at Elisabeth's room. Once inside, she shut the door, let out a huge breath, and they broke into a fit of hushed giggles.

Fiona's mouth fell open as she looked around. "Is this your room? I have *never* seen anything this grand before." She put the basket of food on the floor and then threw herself onto the bed.

Elisabeth plopped down beside her. "It's really nice but...I need to find a way to get back home. My parents are probably losing their minds with worry." Her voice choked with tears. "I *have* to find out how I got here."

"Well...what do you remember last?"

Elisabeth sat up, shaking her head repeatedly. "It was just my mom and I. We had pizza and watched a movie."

"*All right...*" Fiona said in an uncertain tone, clearly not knowing what either pizza or a movie were.

"I fell asleep on the couch." Her eyes narrowed. "The last thing I remember was my dad coming home from work. He carried me up to bed and tucked me in. I fell back to sleep and that's when this nightmare began." Elisabeth looked up, giving Fiona a pained stare. "No offense, it's not that you're a nightmare. It's just...I'm scared. What if I never find out how to get back home? What if I never see my family again?"

"You will," Fiona said in a soothing tone. "You got here somehow, so that means there has to be a way for you to get back again. Was there anything you did differently? There must be something different, something new?" She rolled onto her side.

Elisabeth's head jerked back. "This necklace is new. I was at home, in my bed, and—"

As she twirled the crystal in her fingers, everything around her turned to darkness.

It felt like she was falling.

She squeezed her eyes shut and all the colors of the universe seemed to flash in front of her and then, all at once, the motion stopped.

****

Elisabeth froze, afraid to open her eyes. Everything smelled familiar. It wasn't possible, was it? She opened her eyes and then covered her mouth with both hands. She was lying down beneath a cozy blanket. Her cozy blanket! She was home! She was home, in her room, in her bed.

It was nighttime.

But...the house was quiet.

Too quiet.

Her brows squished together in confusion. As a twelve-year-old girl who'd vanished from her bed the night before, she'd half expected to find complete chaos: flashing police lights, news cameras, and everyone in Mahone Bay searching for her.

Elisabeth threw off the covers and rushed from the room, desperate to tell everyone she was okay. "Mom? Dad?"

She marched down the hall, knocking once before throwing the door wide open.

She crossed the bedroom and was surprised to see her parents were sound asleep…rather peacefully too.

"I'm home," she whispered, shaking her father's shoulder repeatedly. "I'm home."

"What's the matter, princess?" he mumbled in his sleep. "Go back to bed. I *just* tucked you in…" His voice trailed off.

Elisabeth's eyes widened and she looked over at her father's alarm clock.

Eleven-fifteen p.m.

Had no time passed since she'd left?

Mother sat up and yawned. "What's wrong, sweetie? Did you have a bad dream?"

Elisabeth shuffled back a step. "Yeah. It…" Her shoulders slumped, realizing none of it had been real. "Yeah, I…I had a weird dream. Nighty-night."

With a heavy sigh, she shuffled back to her room.

Chapter Seven

The next morning, a spring breeze flapped Elisabeth's bedroom curtains. Warmth radiated through her body and she rolled over, still snuggled beneath the comforter. Her gaze drifted from hairbands, barrettes, and brushes atop her dresser, to the backpack leaning against the wall beside the door. It was so different from the bedroom at Castle Ealasaid.

Suddenly, a heavy feeling washed over her. Castle Ealasaid had been nothing more than a dream.

But...

It was *so* vivid.

Elisabeth sat up and softly shook her head, recalling every little detail about her day in Scotland; from Malcom and the boar, to Fiona, Quinton, and Dandy. Her brows pulled in, wondering how Fiona could be anything but real. The Scottish girl certainly felt like more than a figment of an overactive imagination.

Elisabeth climbed out of bed and began pacing. Of course it was all a dream. Magic isn't real and a person can't travel through time, either.

But...

There *was* one way to find out for sure and put the matter to rest.

She bit her nails.

Finally, Elisabeth closed her eyes, twirling the stone in her fingers while thinking about Fiona.

The light around her faded to black.

She was falling, falling…

****

"Dinnae you fret. We'll figure out a way to get you home."

Elisabeth's pulse raced when hearing that thick Scottish accent once again. She opened her eyes and froze while glancing around the room. It remained exactly the same as when she left. It was still night outside. Fiona was still stretched on her side.

Elisabeth reached out, grabbing her friend's arm. "It did work! It worked, Fee! Did nothing change here? I wasn't gone?"

Wide-eyed, Fiona sat up and shook her head.

Elisabeth jumped up, unable to keep still. "I've been at home the entire night."

"What do you mean you've been home the entire night?" She leaned closer. "You've not left my side."

"My parents said they had just tucked me in and told me to go back to sleep. I thought this was all a dream. I spent last night in my bed at home in my room." Excitement pulsed through her. "I don't know how it works, but I think time stands still while I'm gone."

Fiona gasped as Elisabeth bounced from foot to foot.

"Hang on. Let's see if I can do it again. It seems way too easy. I'll let you know what happens this time. This is *so* cool."

Elisabeth closed her eyes and thought of home while holding the pendant.

She knew it was working.

She could feel it.

****

Seconds later, Elisabeth stood in her own room once more. She grabbed the sides of her head, squealing.

It felt like she held the power of the universe on a chain around her neck. Oh, this was too awesome to be true. It had to be the coolest thing any twelve-year-old owned…or *anyone* owned, for that matter.

"Breakfast," her mother hollered from downstairs "Do you want some pancakes?"

"Yes! I'm starving." She hopped down the steps two at a time, entered the kitchen, and gobbled everything up. Her mom couldn't make them fast enough.

Elisabeth's entire body quivered, trying to control her excitement. She wanted to tell her parents everything. They would never believe her. If they did, they'd never, in a million years, let her go gallivanting on the other side of the world, and definitely not three hundred and fifty years in the past. She wasn't even allowed to go to the mall by herself yet. With a fluttery feeling in her chest, she knew she'd have to keep this to herself.

"Eat up. We have to leave in twenty minutes."

Elisabeth gasped.

Mom did a double-take. "You forgot you had ballet?"

"I forgot it was Saturday," she said, adding more maple syrup to her pancakes. "They should teach ballet in gym class instead of baseball."

A little over an hour later, she was home again,

changing out of her leotard. Her mom busied herself painting while Dad spoke on the phone to a worried patient. This would be the perfect time to slip away for some fun. It was still night in Scotland, so Elisabeth put her nightgown back on. Once morning came, she'd dress in something from the armoire. She couldn't exactly show up in seventeenth century Scotland dressed like a twenty-first-century kid.

Excited, Elisabeth wanted to bring something back to show Fiona it was all true. She grabbed her backpack, dancing around the house, looking for things to show her friend. She dropped in an old smartphone her parents let her "play" with. It had games and music on it, a flashlight, camera, but not much else. It didn't matter. Fiona would be astonished. Deciding to stay in Scotland for the day, nobody at home would even realize she was gone.

After checking to make sure the coast was clear, Elisabeth went to the kitchen and made two peanut butter and jam sandwiches, wanting to avoid the food there as much as possible. She found a candy bar in the cupboard and tossed it into the bag as well, wondering if Fiona had ever tasted chocolate. A copy of *Anne of Green Gables* and a magazine found on a table were tossed in next. Unable to think of anything else to bring, she went back to her room. There, Elisabeth slung the backpack over her shoulder and closed her eyes while twirling the crystal in her fingers.

****

Fiona's mouth dropped. To her, a bag appeared, as if by magic, over Elisabeth's shoulder. "How long were you gone this time?"

"A few hours. I had breakfast with my parents. I

60

went to my ballet class and…look, I even brought some things back to show you. It's true. It's all true. Isn't this amazing and wonderful all at the same time?"

Fiona moved closer. "I don't even know what to say. This is incredible."

"Have you ever had chocolate?" Elisabeth asked.

"Chocolate?" A slow smile built. "No, but I've heard of it. Dinnae tell me you have some?"

"I brought some for you to try." After unwrapping the bar, she handed a piece to Fiona. "Here."

"I thought you were supposed to drink chocolate?" Fiona said.

"Oh, well, yeah, you can drink hot chocolate or chocolate milk, but this is a chocolate bar. There are so many different kinds. Don't bite it. Let it melt on your tongue." Elisabeth's posture relaxed after placing a square on her tongue. "Mmm. Isn't it great? I *love* chocolate."

Fiona's eyes were bright and glossy while savoring her piece. "Elisabeth…" She let out an appreciative sigh. "That was the best thing I ever ate in my entire life."

"Do you want another piece?"

"Aye…please." Fiona grabbed another square as fast as she could. "Oh…" She held her breath, relishing the second piece. "This is *awfully* good."

"Here, Fee…" Elisabeth couldn't help giggling. "Have the whole thing."

Although Fiona shook her head, she couldn't take her eyes off it. "No, I cannae take your chocolate—"

"I insist." Elisabeth placed the remainder into Fiona's outstretched hand and then gave her a playful nudge. "Now, wait until you see what else I have to show you."

Fiona's smile wavered. "I really, really, have to go home now…even though I don't want to yet. I'll try and come back as soon as I can tomorrow. Will you promise to show me then?"

"Oh, sure. Of course." Elisabeth clasped her hands in her lap. "You should go. I'll see you in the morning and show you some more neat stuff."

Fiona pressed both palms to her cheeks. "I know I won't sleep at all tonight wondering what's in your sack."

The girls tiptoed back down the hall and said their hushed goodbyes. Elisabeth once again lifted the heavy latch onto the door and crept back upstairs to her bedroom. She lay down in the large bed under the heavy canopy, trying to sleep until Castle Ealasaid was awake and bustling with activity.

But sleep wouldn't come.

Since she'd spent the night at home, it felt like the middle of the afternoon. Time seemed to stand still in one century, while she was in the other. Taking out the smart phone, she played some games on it and read from her book for a bit. With a sigh, she sat in the window, gazing out into the darkness.

In the magnificent moonlit trees, she could see the flickering of fireflies. As they winked on and off, Elisabeth watched. It reminded her of the time she was camping on the Glooscap Trail with her family several summers ago, at the age of eight.

One night, she had wandered away from her older cousin, and onto the campsite of an intriguing and mysterious man. He sat in a comfortable chair with his back to the trees. As he stared into the fire, Elisabeth stood watching him. The man was nothing more than a shadow in the darkness, except for brief moments when light from the dancing flames lit up his face.

Her breathing slowed, as if a flood of memories about him were trying to take over.

"Hello, Elisabeth," he said quietly.

Tilting her head to the side, she crept closer. "How do you know my name?"

"Because…" Leaning forward, a slight smile lit up his face. "I'm magic."

Wide-eyed, Elisabeth moved even closer. "You're magic?"

"Well, I have powers that are *like* magic." The man paused for a moment. "Do you want to know a secret?"

Elisabeth nodded.

"So do you. In fact, we all have magical powers, but we've forgotten."

She suddenly became still, hanging on his every word.

"Always remember that," he said with a soft voice.

With rapt attention, she planted herself at his feet.

"You should run along." He pulled at his ear. "I don't want you to worry your parents."

"It's okay," her posture relaxed. "My cousin told them where I am," she lied.

With a subdued laugh, the man softly shook his head. He then let out a dejected sigh and ended up telling her swashbuckling stories; tales of a gladiator named Aquarius, runaway slaves, and a brave princess—until Elisabeth's frantic parents found her a short time later, after her cousin returned without her. But, instead of leaving, the man invited her parents to join him around the fire. Soon, they too were mesmerized by him.

He gave Elisabeth a jar and taught her how to use a flashlight to catch fireflies. She ran around the campsite for quite a while, filling the glass until there was a significant amount flickering inside of it. Then, she returned to the man and sat at his feet while he continued to captivate everyone.

Opening the jar, the man, with delicate fingers, removed a firefly. With great care, he squished the beetle in his fingers, and then peeled the glowing light off the bug to reveal a powder-like substance. He rubbed the powder onto Elisabeth's face in an Indian war-paint pattern. The powder continued to glow and flicker on her face, blinking on and off, on and off, for at least another half hour. With a feeling of weightlessness, she danced around the fire, her face and arms glowing and flashing in a variety of colors. Twinkling firefly butts smeared all over her. After saying goodnight, she realized not only did she not know his name, she never really saw his face in the darkness. That didn't matter. She'd never forget him—for there was something magical about that evening.

Now, her eyes inexplicably prickled with tears as she watched the fireflies. After recalling the encounter with that strange, enchanting man, Elisabeth's hands clutched together. She suddenly wanted to catch them like she had that warm summer night. Grabbing the candle lantern from the table, she wrapped a blanket around her nightgown and tiptoed out of the castle and into the night.

Crickets chirped as she marched across the courtyard, through the dew-laced grass, and then to the trees. Elisabeth put her lantern on the ground, and perched on the swing, watching for the flickering lights. Spotting one, she went in for the capture, trapping a little insect in her cupped hands. Elisabeth wrinkled her nose, took a deep breath, and then squished the bug. She peeled the light off its bottom and smeared it on her face. Arms held out wide, as if hugging the world, she danced around the trees, easily catching more and more fireflies.

Elisabeth continued painting herself with their flickering lights before returning to the wooden swing. She pumped her legs, swinging higher and higher until a feeling of breathlessness took over. This whole new world was better than Christmas morning. She jumped off the swing, grabbed her lantern, and danced all the way back to the castle while blinking and twinkling on and off.

Suddenly, her body tensed and she glanced around, wide-eyed. When the hair lifted on the back of her neck, Elisabeth stared into the darkness, feeling certain someone was watching her. With a pounding heart, she sprinted the remainder of the way, pulled the door open, quickly latching it behind her. Once safe within the castle walls, she let out a sigh of relief and climbed the staircase, wondering what glorious things tomorrow would hold.

Chapter Eight

John took off his hat and ran a trembling hand through his hair. Hoping it looked suitable, he licked his palm, trying to flatten the cowlick at the back of his head. He took a deep breath, knocked on the door, and tried to stop his knees from shaking, but the butterflies in his stomach were doing loopy-loops now, too.

Sarah's eyes widened while answering the door. "John? What are you doing here?"

"Good morning, Sarah. Um, I was wondering, uh…is your father home?"

Her brow wrinkled. "My father? Yeah…" she said with a slight nod. "Why are you all dressed up?"

John cleared his throat. "May I please speak to Mr. Floyd?"

Both hands flew to her chest and then a huge smile swept across her face. "Father!" she yelled, continuing to stand in the doorway.

While the two waited in uncomfortable silence for her father, John stared at his feet and rolled the rim of his hat with shaky fingers. Sarah still wore an enormous grin and looked everywhere except at John.

Seconds ticked by as if they were hours.

"John, come in, come in," Mr. Floyd said. "What can I do for you, young man?" He took a seat in his chair and lit his pipe. Sarah excused herself by announcing she needed to sweep the small porch.

John crossed and uncrossed his arms while standing. "Well, um, Mr. Floyd, I was wondering if I, that is, I would be, uh—"

"Spit it out, boy."

John closed his eyes and let the words tumble out as fast as they could in order to get this ordeal over with. "Might-you-be-so-inclined-to-give-me-permission-for-Sarah's-hand-in-marriage?"

Mr. Floyd didn't answer. He sat in silence, puffing on his pipe. "Sit down, John," he finally said.

With a sluggish heartbeat, John took a seat.

"How old are you, son?"

"I'm sixteen, sir. I'll be seventeen in the winter."

"Well, John, I have no doubt you love my daughter."

"Very much, sir."

"And I love him, too, Father!" Sarah yelled from outside.

"But you see, son, I'm a practical man so I don't want to hear all about the love in your heart because that won't put food on the table and a roof over her head. I want to know how it is you plan to support my daughter."

"Well, sir, I hadn't thought of that yet. I, uh…"

"Tell you what. You're a good kid, and I like your father. You come back someday when you have land of your own—"

"But, Father—" Sarah appeared in the doorway.

"Sarah, enough! This matter doesn't concern you." He sat back and puffed on his pipe again. "Where was I, boy?"

"You were saying when I have—"

"Ah, yes, you come back when you have land to build a home for her and she's all yours. If you still want her, that is."

Sarah gasped. "Father!"

Mr. Floyd stood and held out his hand, indicating the meeting was finished.

John wiped a sweaty palm on his pants. "Yes, sir." He shook Mr. Floyd's hand. "Thank you, sir."

Sarah's father showed him the door, which slammed behind him. Once outside, he sighed and put his hat back on. His betrothal was over before it even began.

****

Dawn finally came with the promise of another beautiful day. Elisabeth peered out her window, in awe of the sunbeams streaming through the clouds while lighting up the heavens. The sky here in the Highlands seemed different from home; it appeared lower, as if reaching down to touch the rugged landscape.

The smell of bacon and eggs wafted into her room on the warm breeze, causing her stomach to rumble. She should start getting dressed for breakfast. Elisabeth walked to the wardrobe, threw open its doors, and studied the selection of skirts. She pulled a leine over her head and then added her stay, stockings, and shoes. Trying to decide what outer garments to wear, Elisabeth settled on a striped petticoat under a blue skirt, an apron, a pale yellow jacket, and of course, a neckerchief to finish off the ensemble. While tying her long hair back with the red ribbon, she wondered whose clothes these were.

When dressed and ready, Elisabeth exited her room in search of the food that smelled so good. With a sigh of relief, she found Quinton seated at the long table in the main hall and grabbed the chair next to him. A feast set out; her nose hadn't deceived her. She spied some eggs and what resembled bacon.

"Today is going to be an *awesome* day," she said with a deep, gratifying sigh while peeling a hard-boiled egg.

Quinton's eyes twinkled with mischief. "Is that so?"

With a crisp nod, Elisabeth took a bite of bacon. "Yup."

"Tell me…" The boy's lips twitched as he looked down at his plate. "Did you enjoy riding my horse yesterday?"

A smile lit up her face. "Yes! It was amazing. I couldn't—"

"The thing is"—Quinton turned, now glaring at her—"it is a crime, punishable by hanging, to *steal* a horse."

Elisabeth's head jerked back.

Quinton's nostrils flared and his breathing became heavy. "I could have you locked in the tolbooth for what you did…you *and* Fiona."

"What's…?" A heavy feeling filled her stomach. "What's a tolbooth?"

"It's where criminals go," Quinton said with an exaggerated eye roll. "Before they hang."

Elisabeth's hands trembled. How could she be so stupid? She should never have gone riding with Fiona. Maybe this was the same as if, in her time, they had stolen a car and taken it for a joyride. People got locked up in dark, dirty, damp dungeons for something like twenty years for stealing a loaf of bread in the old days.

And here she was, smack dab in the middle of the old days. They were going to sentence her to hang for stealing a horse.

Although beginning to like this place, now she would have to use her crystal necklace to leave and never return. Elisabeth's chest caved in. "I don't want to die," she whispered, her voice choked with tears.

Quinton burst into laughter.

Elisabeth's mouth opened, but nothing came out.

"I'm teasing. Do you honestly think I care if you and Fiona rode Dandy? On the contrary, I love watching Fiona get the better of old Joseph. He's mean as a viper."

She gave Quinton an incredulous look. "That was *so* mean."

He shrugged. "Nah, you can ride Dandy whenever you want."

Elisabeth let out a huge breath. Part of her wanted to reach over and smack him like Fiona did the day before. "I'm going to get even with you for that," she said with a shaky laugh. "So you better watch your back."

"We'll see," he said with a bemused smile. "We'll see."

"What are you doing this morning?"

"I have lessons to attend after breakfast. Hopefully, I'll have some time with you and Fiona later."

After Elisabeth finished eating, she decided to explore the grounds some more. She walked out of the castle and into the warm sunshine. It was bright and early, yet people were already going about their daily tasks and chores.

Off the main courtyard, Elisabeth found a path she

had not yet traveled. Flanked on both sides by a wide perennial border, tiny flowers lining the edge spilled onto the walkway, while spikey delphinium and foxglove blooms along the back stood taller than she was. Dark pink rose bushes, appearing to be in their first glorious flush, perfumed the air. Ahead, a squirrel skittered beneath a stone arch, leading Elisabeth into what appeared to be the entrance of a walled kitchen garden. Inside were neat rows of herbs and vegetables; round cabbages and frilly carrot tops. As she walked by an old wheelbarrow, a dragonfly landed on the handle. Her posture relaxed thinking how much her mother would love to paint this scene. Abby London adored gardens and this one was the epitome of charming. She raised her eyebrows, spotting a wall of evergreen hedges to her right, with a large wooden door in the center.

A wide grin spread across her face. Elisabeth rushed over and rattled the handle. The door was locked. She took a step back wondering what was beyond it. Her hand covered her mouth realizing it probably hid a secret garden, the kind she'd only read about in old books. She tried the handle again.

No luck.

While tapping her foot, she glanced around, looking for another way in.

Nope.

She'd definitely find out what was hidden behind the locked door later.

Elisabeth exited the walled kitchen garden through an open gate opposite the stone arch. From there, the path meandered into some trees, their leaves rustling in the breeze.

A pesky little fly decided to accompany her. As it buzzed by one ear, she kept swatting it away. The more she shook her head, the more it persisted. Apparently, it also had friends. Instead of leaving her alone, it brought backup.

The buzzing grew louder and louder. Elisabeth walked with jerky movements, still unable to get away from the growing swarm of little gnats. She gritted her teeth, eventually screaming, "Stop it!" with a theatrical groan while swatting them away.

They continued their torment.

As Elisabeth stormed down the path, Malcolm appeared.

"These things are driving me crazy!" she yelled.

His eyes bulged as he neared. "You have an *entire* halo of midges around your head, lass."

"Is that what they are…?" Her nostrils flared. "They won't leave me alone."

"Well, it's obvious they like you." Malcolm chuckled as he continued in the opposite direction. "If you're looking for wee Fiona, she's down at the loch," he shouted over his shoulder.

"*Where?*" Elisabeth asked, still swatting at her head, jumping up and down.

"Follow the path, lassie."

Elisabeth broke into a sprint, waving her arms in the air while trying to outrun the bugs. Shona, who was walking by, stopped and watched in bewilderment as Elisabeth went flying past her.

A few minutes later, she burst out of the trees and could see a lake shimmering ahead. Fiona was crouched at the shore, engaged in some chore.

"Hi, Fee," she shouted. "Want some help?"

Fiona looked up with a huge smile. "That would be awfully nice. I have to fill these creels with seaweed." She pointed by nodding her nose in the direction of some baskets. "It won't take too long." Her eyes then widened. "Oh my word, look at you. Those midges are all over you."

"I know! They're driving me crazy. They must like my shampoo or something."

"How did you know I was here?"

"Your future husband, Malcolm, told me you were at the *loch*." Elisabeth exaggerated the pronunciation of the word. "I don't know what a *loch* is, but I'm guessing it's a lake?"

Fiona burst into laughter. "Aye, this is a *loch*."

The gnats eventually left and the two girls filled the baskets with seaweed. When finished, Elisabeth insisted on helping Fiona carry them to her cottage. They left the baskets beside the garden and snuck away before Mrs. McAllistair could call Fiona back to do more chores.

"What's behind the hedges with that locked door I saw near the vegetable garden?" Elisabeth asked as they strolled back toward the castle.

"It's a maze."

Her lips parted. "A maze? Can we go in?"

"Of course. Quinton and I like to race through it." Fiona broke out into a wide grin. "Say...if you bring down your sack, we can look at everything you brought once we get to the center."

"Good idea," Elisabeth said, bouncing on her tiptoes.

Fiona's expression suddenly softened once they entered the main courtyard. "I'll wait for you right here," she murmured.

Elisabeth followed her friend's gaze and realized she was watching Malcolm talk to someone. "Do you want me to take my time?" she asked with a snort.

Fiona's head tilted to the side. "Do you think he'll wait for me to grow up and marry me someday?"

Elisabeth gave her a playful pinch. "I suppose you could dare to dream." With that, she ran inside the castle and up to her room, retrieving her backpack.

When she returned, the two strolled along the path through the garden, and to the door nestled into the wall of evergreen hedges. With a grin that seemed to convey secret knowledge, Fiona bent down to move a rock.

"The key's hidden under here," she whispered.

A moment later, Fiona unlocked the door with an old brass key before putting it back again.

Adrenaline rushed through Elisabeth's body as the door creaked open. Straight ahead was a wall of shrubbery with a dirt path running left and right in front of it. A smile spread across her face. "Do you know which way to go?"

"Of course," Fiona said, taking wide steps to the left before disappearing around the corner. "Follow me." She broke into a run, weaving her way through the labyrinth, giggling as Elisabeth tried to keep up. "This way…" she'd call out from behind the next turn.

After losing Fiona a few times, and getting completely turned around, Elisabeth eventually stepped out onto an intimate courtyard edged with four benches. A stone fountain in the center was filled with rainwater in which two small birds played. With a satisfied sigh, she looked up. The only thing visible over the hedge was part of the castle and the sky above.

"We should come here every day," Elisabeth said, taking a seat on one of the benches.

"Aye." Fiona took a deep breath. "It's bonnie, isn't it?"

"You know..." Elisabeth dug through her backpack after her stomach growled. "I don't suppose you've ever had a peanut butter and jam sandwich, have you?"

Fiona leaned forward, shaking her head.

"Do you want to try one?"

"Aye," she said, smoothing down her skirt. "If it's anything like the chocolate you gave me, I'm more than happy to oblige."

Elisabeth unwrapped the sandwiches and handed one to Fiona, who took it with as much care as if being handed a fragile little creature.

"Mmm, try it," Elisabeth urged while taking a bite of her own. "It's really good. I didn't realize I was so hungry."

Fiona's nose wrinkled and she took the tiniest nibble, causing Elisabeth to burst into laughter, unsure whether she liked it or not.

"It has a strange taste I'm not used to..." She took a few more little nibbles. "Sorry. I like the chocolate much, much better." Her eyebrows pinched together and she handed Elisabeth the remainder of the sandwich. "Here, you finish it."

With a bemused smile, Elisabeth snatched the sandwich back and polished that one off as well. "Okay. Fee...are you ready to see some really cool stuff?"

She bit down on a smile and nodded. "Aye."

Elisabeth placed the old smartphone into Fiona's

hand. "Guess what this does?"

She leaned forward, examining it. "Well, it doesn't feel cold. It feels rather warm. When does it get cold?"

"Huh?"

"You said you had cold things to show me."

Elisabeth burst into laughter before explaining a new meaning of the word *cool* to her seventeenth-century companion. "Remember when I asked if you or Quinton had a phone I could borrow?"

Fiona nodded.

"Well, at home we use this to talk to other people over long distances. I was hoping you had one so I could talk to my parents."

Fiona's body stiffened.

"Plus, there are entire libraries you can access. You can read any book or find an answer to just about any single question you might have. Unfortunately, I can't do any of that here though, it won't work. But...it plays music. I put all my favorite songs on it so I can listen to them whenever I want. Here." She put the earphones into her friend's ears and chose a song for her to listen to.

Fiona gave a slow, disbelieving shake of her head. "How does it work?"

Elisabeth shrugged her shoulders. "That's too complicated to explain. And besides, I've got more stuff to show you."

She loaded a game and demonstrated how to play it. Fiona sucked in a quick breath and then proceeded to play for the better part of an hour while Elisabeth read her book. She didn't want to spoil her fun. It was clearly incredible to see things like that for the first time in your life when you're not even used to indoor plumbing or electricity yet.

"You really *are* from the twenty-first century," Fiona said with a spontaneous laugh as she looked up from the smartphone.

Elisabeth held her chin high. "Yep."

"What is it like? I mean, what is the world like? After seeing this, I cannot even imagine it."

Her brow wrinkled. "I don't even know where to begin. Let's see. We don't use horses like you do here anymore. I mean...we *have* horses, but cars were invented and, oh...how do I explain it? A car is like a carriage that doesn't need a horse to pull it. It can go fast, way faster than a horse, and everyone travels by car. Did you know you can also travel even faster in the sky in an airplane?"

Fiona shook her head in disbelief.

"You can fly places in the future," Elisabeth continued. "It's like a big carriage with huge wings on the sides. People sit inside it and it can fly you across the world in hours."

"Do the wings flap?"

"No, they don't flap. They stay still." Elisabeth grabbed her backpack and took out the magazine she'd thrown in there earlier. "Maybe this has pictures..." She flipped through and saw it was loaded with advertisements and lots of photographs. "It does! So...this is a washing machine and a dryer." She pointed to one of the glossy pages. "You put your dirty clothes inside, push the buttons, and your clothes get washed. When it's done, you put it in the other machine and it dries them."

Fiona pointed to a picture on another page and gasped. "Is that what people dress like? Is that a girl?

Oh my goodness…" She leaned in closer. "Is that what you wear?"

"Oh, yeah, we can wear pants or skirts or dresses or pretty much anything we want. Long or short. Whatever."

Fiona pointed to a picture of a sink and a faucet. "What's that?"

"Water comes out of there. You turn those knobs for hot or cold water."

"Is that what your lochs look like in the future?" she asked, pointing to a lady in a swimming pool.

Elisabeth chuckled. "We swim in those. Oh, look, there. I found a picture of a car." She pointed to an ad featuring a shiny silver automobile.

Fiona was so amazed by everything that she sat and poured over the magazine for a long, long time, asking Elisabeth to explain each and every item.

"Fiona? Elisabeth?"

The girls stared at each other wide-eyed when they heard Quinton coming through the maze, hollering their names.

"The door was open. Are you in here? Fee-oh-nah?"

Elisabeth jumped up, bouncing on her toes. "Here…" she said quietly. "Give me my stuff. Don't let Quinton see it yet."

Fiona helped to stuff the smartphone, book, and magazine into the backpack. "You don't think we should tell Quinton about where, er…*when*, you're from?" she whispered.

"Not yet. Quick…" Elisabeth ran with the backpack, hiding it in one of the hedges.

"Awww, now our fun is ruined for Quinton is

here," Fiona said with a smirk as he stepped into the center of the maze to join the girls.

"What are you doing?" He glanced around while the girls stood swinging their arms by their sides.

"Nothing. We were just talking," said Elisabeth.

"You look like you're both up to something." A slow smile built. "What are you *really* doing?"

"Really. We're just standing here," Fiona said.

Elisabeth let out an exaggerated sigh. "If you *must* know, I was showing Fee a magic trick."

"A magic trick?" Quinton crossed his arms. "*You* know a magic trick?"

Fiona swallowed her laughter. "Oh, she is *very* good at magic tricks."

"Really?" He shot Elisabeth a sidelong glance. "Can I see?"

"I don't know…" She rubbed her chin.

Quinton's eyes widened. "Seriously?"

Elisabeth exhaled heavy, pretending to give in. "Fine." She clamped her lips together, trying not to laugh while walking right up to him. "All right…" With dramatic flair, she waved her arms in the air. "Abracadabra. Hocus pocus…"

Elisabeth slipped one hand behind her back, and with the other hand, held her crystal necklace.

Thoughts of home on her mind.

Home.

****

Within a moment, she was back in her bedroom. As she ran downstairs, her eyes widened, and she cursed under her breath, realizing she was still in her old-fashioned clothing. Unsure how'd she explain that, her shoulders tightened, watching as her father spoke on the phone. With his back to her, she tiptoed, as silently as possible, to the kitchen. She grabbed a paper plate and took a can of whipped cream out of the fridge before sneaking back up to her room.

Her body quaked from trying not to laugh as she sprayed the entire contents of the can onto the plate, ending up with a huge, overflowing dish of whipped cream. Then, with a deep breath, she stood in the exact same position she had been in when disappearing from the Highlands. One hand clutched her necklace, the other one tucked behind her back...this time, holding the loaded paper plate.

She rubbed the crystal with her free hand, knowing, within seconds, she'd be back in the middle of the garden maze, standing in front of Quinton.

****

"Ready?" she asked him.

"Aye."

Quinton never saw the pie in the face coming.

He yelped and shuffled back a step while wiping the cream out of his eyes. He then broke out into a fit of laughter, trying to lick the parts of his face his tongue could reach. "This tastes delicious. What is it?"

"It's whipped cream," Elisabeth said, dissolving into giggles herself. "And that's payback for threatening to send me to the tolbooth."

Fiona gasped. "You threatened to send her to the tolbooth?"

"Yeah." Elisabeth gave her an incredulous look. "For stealing his horse."

"Quinton!" She shot him a wide-eyed stare that caused everyone to break into laughter again.

"I was only joking." He sucked in a quick breath,

moving closer to Elisabeth. "How did you do that? That was brilliant. You *must* teach me that trick."

She shook her head. "A good magician never reveals how her tricks are done."

"You *have* to tell me." He was jumping up and down. "That was the best trick I've ever seen before. I didn't see it behind your back. It was fantastic."

Elisabeth's brows pulled in as she looked at Fiona. "Do you think we should tell him the truth?"

Fiona shrugged her shoulders. "It's up to you. He *can* keep a secret though, can't you, Quinton?"

He was unnaturally still. "Aye."

"But..." Elisabeth pursed her lips. "This is a big one."

"Huge," Fiona added.

"Trust me. I can keep a secret."

Elisabeth jerked her head back when Fiona ran full speed at Quinton and tackled him. She was smaller than he was, but it took him by surprise, propelling him flat on his back, Fiona landing on top.

"Quinton, if you tell anyone this secret we're about to tell you, you're going to be sorry. Swear on your life you won't tell."

"I promise. I promise." His eyes widened and shot Fiona a look as if she had gone mad.

Fiona stood, and while she brushed the dust off her skirt, Quinton also stood, looking ready to promise anything under the sun, as long as he was in on the secret too.

Elisabeth softly shook her head, struggling to find the right words. "I'm...well...you see—"

"She's from the future," Fiona blurted out before squealing dramatically. "The twenty-first century."

Quinton burst into laughter again. "Don't tell me you believe that, Fee? You might as well believe in St. Columba's water monster in the River Ness, too."

"It's true. Show him your stuff," Fiona said. "He'll keep your secret, won't you, Quinton?"

When Elisabeth pulled out her smartphone and loaded a game for him to play, he let out a small yelp.

Quinton, too, was now a believer.

Fiona and Elisabeth filled him in on all the details of her crystal necklace.

Spring turned into summer, and the three friends were inseparable. Elisabeth wished it could stay this way forever. She loved showing Fiona and Quinton things they had never even dreamed of, and telling them stories about the future. Days were simple and carefree—from riding Dandy through the meadow to playing in the shadowy halls of the old castle.

Elisabeth's presence became a fixed and welcome feature at Castle Ealasaid. Lady McQuade and Malcolm accepted her as part of their family, with surprisingly few questions asked. When Elisabeth went home to be with her family, time stood still in Scotland, and when she returned to Ealasaid, everything stopped at home. She was free to explore and pass the days in the Highlands. It didn't interfere with her school work or home life. On the contrary, time was something she had in abundance. It was like having a forty-eight-hour day and living two simultaneous lives.

Sometimes, when Quinton had to leave and see to his studies, the girls would lie in the grass while Elisabeth read books, like *Anne of Green Gables* or *The Secret Garden*, out loud to her friend. Not only did Fiona not know how to read, she'd never had a book read to her either, except from the bible at church.

"My parents dinnae own any books." Fiona laced her fingers behind her head while watching the clouds float by.

Elisabeth's mouth fell open. "They don't?"

"Not a single one. But once, during a special feast at Ealasaid, a storyteller performed tales and sang songs." Fiona's face lit up at the memory. Her eyes widened and she sat up. "It must be amazing to be able to read."

Elisabeth's brow furrowed. "I never thought about it much."

"Perhaps I'll learn someday." Fiona smiled as she lay back down in the grass, waiting for the story to continue. "Because if I was rich, I'd own all the books that money could buy."

Chapter Nine

Discouraged by his lack of success with both Mr. Floyd and the treasure hunt, John decided to walk along the beach to clear his head. When he got to the water's edge, he found David Perrier staring into the bay with an unfocused gaze. John joined him, silent as they both watched small waves ripple against the rocky shore.

"Hey…" John said, eventually breaking the silence. "I never got the chance to thank you and Samuel for helping us fill the pit back in. Sorry about my father."

"Not a problem at all." David's golden brown hair fell onto his forehead as he looked down at his hands, inspecting several thin, smooth stones. "Is that the end of your treasure hunt, then?"

John's shoulders slumped. "I don't know. Nothing's going right."

"What's the matter?"

"If only I could recover what's buried there, everything would be fine. My life would be perfect."

David let out a heavy sigh. "Be careful not to fall into that trap, my friend. It can be as deadly as your pit."

"What do you mean?"

"I once chased after a dream, much like you are. I thought I'd only be happy when I had it." David shook his head and then his voice lost all its power. "But I didn't find the happiness I thought I would."

"Really?" John said quietly.

"Far from it." He sent a stone skipping across the surface of the water. "What do you expect to find buried there?"

"Pirate booty." John picked up a stone and chucked it into the water. "We think it's probably Captain Kidd's stash. It's supposed to be buried somewhere around here."

"Pirate booty, huh? Let me ask you something. If you find jewels and gold, what can they afford you that you can't provide without them?"

"I want to marry Sarah."

David's head jerked back. He turned to look at John, his blue eyes narrowing as he shoved both fists into his jacket. "And you need a treasure to do that?"

"No, but...." John cleared his throat. "But her father insists I own land."

"John, you don't need buried treasure to buy land. Just look around you. Samuel's family came here all the way from South Carolina because they were giving it away. I have faith you'll find a way to make your dreams come true...with or without buried treasure. Save your money, buy some land, and grow old with Sarah."

"I suppose you're right," John said with a half-hearted shrug.

"I know I am." David turned his attention back to the water, sending another stone skipping far across the bay. "Grow old with Sarah."

John's eyes widened, watching as David's stone continually skimmed the surface of the water.

"Amazing," he shouted with a bark of laughter. "That last rock was...what...fifty skips?"

"Something like that." David seemed to be holding back tears. "Give me a rock and a sling and I can hit anything," he said, mostly to himself.

John slipped both hands into his pockets, staring into the sea until he suddenly gasped. "Why didn't I think of it before?"

David glanced at him. "Think of what?"

"I have to go. You've given me a brilliant idea."

"Glad I could be of help," he said with a small smile.

A bell over the door announced John's arrival as he walked into Wollenhaupt's General Store. The store took its name from owner Caspar Wollenhaupt, who was also the banker in the community, lending or denying credit to his customers. If a local farmer was short on cash, he was often willing to trade butter or eggs for needed goods.

"John Smith, what a coincidence," the bald man said as he glanced up from a book he was writing in. "Your mother was just here. Can I help you with something?"

"Mr. Wollenhaupt, sir. I really hope so."

"Something troubling you?" he asked as he continued to write, only half-listening to John.

"Well, sir, I hope to buy some land from you."

"I'm listening." He put his pen down and gave John his full attention.

"I want to ask for Sarah Floyd's hand, but I need to own land before her father will let us marry. I don't have a lot of money but—"

"Yes, I see, I see," Mr. Wollenhaupt said, smiling.

He brought out a map that showed the entire town and surrounding areas, broken into numbered lots. "I have the perfect lot, not far from here. It would be ideal for you, and I might be willing to work out an arrangement."

"Mr. Wollenhaupt, I have a certain spot in mind." John pointed to a spot on the map. "That one. Lot number eighteen. You own that, right?"

The man's eyes widened. "Why on earth would you want to buy that piece of land? Heaven's above, John, have you no common sense? You want to bring a young bride there? Isn't there somewhere else more appropriate for a young man and his wife to settle down?"

"Probably, sir, but I have my heart set on that particular spot. It's, um, *sentimental* to me."

Mr. Wollenhaupt shook his head as he pondered John's request. "How much money do you have, son?"

"Seven pounds, ten shillings."

"What a coincidence," he said with a long exhale. "That's exactly how much I'd sell that lot for."

"Really?"

"Why not," he said, shaking his head as though regretting his decision. "It's a fair price."

"Really?" John repeated.

"Come back tomorrow. I'll have the papers ready for you to sign."

"Oh, thank you, Mr. Wollenhaupt, thank you. I'm so happy I could kiss you!"

"Get out of here before I change my mind," he said with a laugh.

"Yes, sir!"

The bell chimed again as John ran out the front

door and all the way to the Floyd household. He hoped Sarah wouldn't object to living on a small, isolated, and supposedly haunted island.

****

Elisabeth and Fiona were outside, giggling quietly beneath an open window. To pass the time, they liked to eavesdrop on Shona, who constantly grumbled to herself while working inside the castle.

"Good morning, Shona."

"Oh, good morning, Shona."

"How are you this fine day?"

"Oh, I'm fine. Thank you for asking. Nobody else ever does."

"That's terrible."

"Aye. It is, it is. What are you going to do today?"

"Me? Why first, I'm going to do the *bloody* laundry. Then I have to go to the *bloody* market with Joseph. Then, the master wants me to—"

With a high-pitched voice, Lady McQuade suddenly joined the conversation. "Am I interrupting something?"

Elisabeth and Fiona both clamped hands over their mouths, trying desperately to stop from laughing out loud so they wouldn't be caught spying.

Shona cleared her throat. "Oh, no, ma'am. Thank you. I was just talking to myself. Will the laird be joining you this morning?"

"He left at dawn to see Mr. Rose about a business matter."

Shona's tone softened. "Mr. Rose again—?"

"Aye. Mr. Rose again."

"His daughter Emily is such a lovely thing. Looks like an angel with that golden hair of hers," Shona said.

"Well…Malcolm has always been fond of fair-haired women." Lady McQuade lowered her voice. "Just between you and me, I think my brother is of a serious mind to ask Emily Rose to marry him."

Fiona and Elisabeth stared at each other, wide-eyed.

"Really?" Shona said.

"Aye. Really," Lady McQuade continued.

"Well, she is certainly a beautiful creature."

"With a good heart, too, although her parents can be rather irritating. I wager Malcolm and Emily will be wed within the year."

Wed within the year.

Fiona sagged against the wall. Her chest then hitched. Holding back obvious sobs, she jumped up, running away as fast as possible

"Fee…wait!"

When Elisabeth finally caught up, Fiona was sitting beside the tree with the swing, her head buried in both knees. She looked up; her face red and puffy from crying.

"Emily Rose. I *hate* that name. That's the ugliest, most vile name I've ever heard in my entire life."

Elisabeth flopped down next to her.

"I know I'm too young to get married…" Her voice choked with tears. "But I don't want him to marry anyone. And did you hear that? Lady McQuade said he likes golden hair." Fiona clutched at her stomach. "I have the blackest hair around."

Elisabeth rubbed her back.

"If I had golden hair, do you think maybe he would wait and marry me when I grow up?" Fiona continued sobbing. "He's supposed to marry *meee*…"

"Fee…" Elisabeth's tone was soothing. "He's not going to wait for you to grow up and marry you just because you suddenly have blonde hair."

Fiona shook her head in denial. "How do you know? What if he does? What if he saw me with a bonnie head of fair hair and I won him over? I'll be marrying age in just a few more years. I'll never know, though. I'm stuck with this horrible dark hair. It's hopeless. My life is over." Her bottom lip trembled. "I'm going to die an old maid. Like Shona."

Elisabeth's posture suddenly perked up. "Hey…wait a minute…what if I told you I could turn your hair a beautiful golden blonde?"

Fiona's hands flew to her chest. "You can change my hair color?"

"Yes! My mom colors her hair every month to hide the gray."

"Really?" Fiona held her breath. She tried to wipe tears away, but all she managed to do was spread the dirt from her hands onto her face.

"Oh my gosh, I'm a genius." Elisabeth jumped up. "I bet I could turn you into such a beauty that Malcolm might actually wait for you."

A dramatic, happy squeal escaped Fiona's lips.

****

Elisabeth was home again, sneaking through mother's bathroom. Her chest tightened as she stared at the box of hair color, trying to convince herself that taking it to help Fiona was serving a higher purpose.

Abby London stockpiled the hair color because she was afraid they would stop making her favorite brand.

"Light golden blonde." Elisabeth cleared her throat before helping herself to a box. "Perfect."

****

With a bunch of hair supplies hidden in a sack, the two girls walked down to the loch. Most days, it was isolated and today was no exception. They sat on its banks while Elisabeth read the directions.

"Okay…this seems easy enough."

Fiona shuffled over, planting herself at Elisabeth's feet. "When Malcolm sees my long, flowing, honey-colored hair, he is going to be mesmerized and forget all about Emily Rose. Forever."

Elisabeth smiled, working the dye into Fiona's hair. "I think we should leave it on as long as possible so it gets really, really blonde."

When it was time to wash it out, Fiona waded into the cold loch, too excited about the outcome to care about the frigid temperature of the water. Afterward, her brows squished together while inspecting the ends of her long tresses. "What do you think?"

Elisabeth tapped an index finger against her lips, staring at Fiona's now brassy-orange hair. "I think it looks good. It's not quite as golden as I'd hoped, but it's *definitely* lighter."

A slow smile grew on Fiona's face. "It is lighter, isn't it?"

"Absolutely," she said with a curt nod. "Now, it doesn't last forever. It will eventually wash out."

Fiona exhaled while looking up. "I cannot *wait* for Malcolm to see it."

"Well, let me towel dry and brush it first. Come here."

Later that afternoon, Elisabeth sat in the swing while Fiona bounced from foot to foot alongside her, both keeping watch over the courtyard for Malcolm's return.

Quinton spotted the girls and marched over, stopping mid-stride when he saw Fiona. "What happened to your hair?"

She held her chin high. "Elisabeth did it. What do you think?"

He shrugged his shoulders. "I liked it the way it was."

"Oh, what do you know, anyhow?" Fiona frowned while stomping away.

Elisabeth jumped off the swing.

"Stop…" Quinton called out. He walked around, sniffing the air like a mischievous puppy. His brows furrowed and then released. "Do you smell what I smell?"

Elisabeth's posture perked up and she took a deep, savoring breath. "Mmm, what is that?"

Fiona took a big whiff and then gasped. "Jonnet's blueberry pies."

Next to the front entrance, a woman was arranging a tray of pies on the ledge of the pony wall. As quickly as she'd appeared, she hurried back down the stairs into the servant's entrance. While cooling off, the breeze carried the aroma of warm blueberries right to the children.

Quinton licked his lips.

Fiona leaned in closer.

And a slow smile spread across Elisabeth's face.

"Pie!" They screamed in unison, racing across the courtyard.

"Hey!" Shona called out from an alcove where she'd been washing laundry in a scrub bucket. "You bairns keep your paws off those. They're nae for you."

"What?" Quinton yelped as he turned around. "We cannot have a piece?"

"No."

Fiona clasped both hands under her chin. "Shona, please...I implore you. I could quite possibly die if you say no to—"

"No."

With a theatrical groan, Fiona clutched her heart and pretended to drop dead.

"Get up, child. I said no. And good heavens, lass, what did you do to your hair?"

Fiona bounced up, thrusting her chest out. "Do you love it?"

"No."

"But...it's beautiful golden hair. I look just like a fair maiden."

"You look like a wild banshee is what you look like, and if I know your mother, she's going to have your hide."

Fiona let out a heavy sigh. "I dinnae even want to think about what my mother will say," she mumbled, leading her friends back toward their favorite tree.

Quinton's shoulders slumped. "They wave hot blueberry pies right under our noses but then won't even let us have any."

"I know." Elisabeth flopped onto the wooden swing again. "And it smells *so* good."

"We should tell her that it's good luck to give it to someone. She's so superstitious she might believe it," Fiona said.

Quinton shuffled his feet. "Who?"

"Or..." Fiona glanced at Elisabeth with wide eyes. "You and I could create a diversion and Quinton could sneak off with one of the pies."

His head jerked back. "Oh, sure. Let *me* be the one who gets in trouble for stealing a pie."

"Wait..." Elisabeth grinned. "I have an idea. Follow me..."

They raced across the courtyard and through the kitchen garden. Outside the maze, Elisabeth fumbled for the key hidden under the rock. She unlocked the door and led the way to the center where her backpack was hidden deep within the evergreen shrubs.

She pulled out the smartphone and opened a voice memo app. "Testing. One, two, three, testing."

Fiona sucked in a quick breath. "What are you doing?"

"Watch..." She hit the play button and they all listened to her voice repeat, "Testing. One, two, three, testing."

Quinton's mouth fell open. "That is nothing short of magic."

Elisabeth nodded and leaned back. "Okay, Quinton, here's what you are going to do..."

Shona was still doing laundry when the children walked by her again, traipsing through the courtyard.

"If you're back scrounging for pie again, I already told you no." Her lips pinched together. "It's not for you bairns."

Quinton moaned. "We're not here for pie. Supper isn't ready yet and we're *so* hungry."

"Perhaps Jonnet has a little bread and water to give us?" Elisabeth asked.

"Stale bread will be fine," Fiona added. "We'll probably die of starvation, but at least the pies will be safe."

Shona let out an exasperated sigh. "Go on now. Find something else to do."

"All right, but just remember, *you* sent us away." Quinton sniffled and wiped imaginary tears.

"Come on, guys." Elisabeth clutched her stomach as they shuffled away.

Shona shook her head, muttering under her breath while scrubbing the linens.

Suddenly, the sounds of rattling chains and moaning filled the air. Shona's hand flew to her chest; she jumped up, glancing all around. The noise was coming from a window above her and getting louder.

"Sho-nahhh, this is the ghost of William MacLauchlan. Sho-nahhh…"

As Shona stood, her voice rose in pitch. "What are you bairns…?" When she turned around to scold them, her mouth fell open, realizing they were no longer in the courtyard.

Fiona was perched on the swing.

Quinton and Elisabeth leaned against the tree trunk.

They were nowhere near the noise.

Shona shuffled back a step, frozen as the ghost spoke again.

"Sho-nahhh. This is the ghost of William MacLauchlan. You must leave me an offering of pie…outside the door to the maze. Do it now and no harm shall come to you. Do it now, Sho-nahhh."

Elisabeth gasped, watching as Shona raced to the pony wall, grabbed a pie, and hurried across the courtyard toward the maze.

"She's actually doing it?" Elisabeth shrieked with a disbelieving voice.

Fiona turned away and burst into laughter. "I told you! She's more superstitious than anyone I know."

When Shona was out of sight, the three children raced back inside the castle to retrieve the smartphone they'd hidden in an open window. Clutching each other for support while breaking into fits of giggles, they made their way toward the garden...where Jonnet's blueberry pie was waiting for them.

The remainder of the day dragged on. Malcolm still hadn't returned.

Fiona shook out her hands. "He's spent the entire day with Emily Nose, hasn't he?"

"Emily Nose." Elisabeth snickered while glancing around uneasily. "I don't know where he is, but I need to go. It's almost suppertime."

"I need to go, too," Fiona said with a heavy sigh.

After saying their goodbyes, Elisabeth glanced behind, watching Fiona weave her way down the lane with a hunched posture.

That's when she saw Malcolm, atop his horse, cantering around a bend in the road.

Adrenaline rushed through her veins. Elisabeth dodged behind a tree trunk, desperate to secretly witness his reaction to Fiona's makeover.

Her breath caught, watching as Malcolm almost rode right by Fiona. That had to be a good sign—him not recognizing her right away. This was Fiona's big chance. Her future was about to change forever. One look at her, with her *almost* golden hair, and Malcolm would forget all about Emily Nose and fall in love with Fiona instead.

Elisabeth gently bit her lip.

Malcolm pulled the reins, bringing his horse to a

stop. "Fiona? Is that you?" His brow wrinkled. "What the devil happened to your hair, lass?"

She looked up with a beaming face. "Do you like it? Elisabeth did it for me."

He gasped, before bursting into a belly laugh. "Good Lord, child…you mean to tell me you did that on purpose?"

Fiona jerked her head back, erupted into tears, and then took off running.

Malcolm's mouth fell open as he watched her disappear down the lane, wailing the entire way. "Was it something I said?" he asked his horse before dismounting.

Feeling emotionally drained herself, Elisabeth tiptoed closer, darting from tree to tree, watching as Fiona ran to an immense trunk, flopped down, and sobbed.

She wasn't there more than a few moments when Malcolm found her.

"Fiona? Are you all right?"

She turned away from him. "Leave me alone. This is all your fault."

"I'm very sorry," he said in a soft voice. "I honestly did not mean to hurt your feelings, lass." He sat beside her, leaning against the tree trunk.

She ignored him.

"Now that I look again, your hair is quite lovely. Elisabeth did it for you?"

"Aye," she said quietly.

"I see."

Elisabeth could see Malcolm wiping a hand over his mouth, trying to stifle a grin.

Fiona sniffled and wiped her nose with the back of

her hand.

Malcolm's head tilted to the side. "Might I ask why you thought you needed to change your hair? I thought it was very pretty black."

Her brows furrowed and then released before looking up at him. "You did?"

"Aye. I always thought you had the finest hair in all of Scotland. Black as night."

Her eyes widened. "I thought you liked golden hair. That's why I changed it."

Malcolm gave her an incredulous stare. "You changed your hair for me? What on earth for, lass?"

Fiona covered her face with both hands as uncontrollable sobs took over. "You're going to marry Emily *Nose*. Everyone knows it." Her voice choked with tears. "You're supposed to wait for me. I want to marry you when I grow up. I know that sounds ridiculous, but it's true. I dinnae want you to marry her. I want you to marry *meee* someday."

Malcolm's posture stiffened, then he pressed a fist against his lips, trying *really* hard not to laugh. "Oh, Fiona, Fiona. I'm not marrying Emily Nose."

She held her breath. "You're not?"

"No. I'm not. Nor am I marrying Emily *Rose*, for that matter."

Fiona sagged against the tree in relief.

"I am much, much, too old for you, but let me tell you; if I was a young lad, say…around Quinton's age…I'd be absolutely mad about you."

Fiona sniffled and wiped her nose with the back of her hand again. "You would?"

"Aye, I would. With your lovely *black* hair."

Neither of them said another word for a few

minutes.

"Well…it'll eventually wash out," she mumbled.

"That's good." He gave her a playful nudge. "Fiona, I've known you since you were a wee babe. I'll always love you, you're part of my clan, but you're going to grow up and marry some devilishly handsome man one day, and I'm going to be old and crippled by then. You'll not want *me* by the time you're ready to pick a husband."

Fiona laid a hand over her heart. "Aye, I will."

He scrunched his face all up and hunched over, holding his hands distorted as if he were a hundred-year-old man.

When Fiona let out a shaky laugh, Malcolm sighed deeply and shot her a thoughtful expression. "Do you feel a *wee* bit better?"

She answered with a small nod.

"Good. Now dry your eyes." He pulled her up to her feet and hugged her. After Fiona let out a long exhale, Malcolm watched her stroll away before adding, "Oh, just so you know, lass, my nephew *is* mad about you."

Fiona's nose scrunched up as she spun around. "He is?"

"Aye, he most certainly is." With a bemused smile, he mounted his horse and then started back toward the castle…before coming to an abrupt stop. "Elisabeth!" he suddenly called out in a sharp tone.

Her hand flew to her chest.

He knew she was there?

Elisabeth cleared her throat. "Yes…?" she answered, still hiding behind the tree.

Malcolm plucked at his clothes as if cooling down.

"You can ride back with me, lass, on one condition…"

Elisabeth shuffled into view, fiddling with her jacket sleeves. "Hmm?"

"Promise you won't touch my hair," he said with a wink.

Chapter Ten

"Morning."

Elisabeth's father looked up with a wide grin. "Good morning, princess."

"You're in a good mood." She smiled, grabbing a dish from the cupboard, a spoon from the drawer, before sitting across from him at the table. "What's up?"

Dad took a sip of his coffee. "Listen to this…" He scrolled through his tablet. "It's about the Money Pit."

"Ohhh…" Elisabeth chuckled while pouring cereal and milk into her bowl. "You're still obsessed with the Money Pit?"

His eyebrows wiggled. "Ever since I was a boy."

"Is it in the news again?"

"It's for sale! Here, let me read it to you." Dad cleared his throat. "NOVA SCOTIA: Looking for a little adventure? The Oak Island Money Pit is for sale. Maybe you will be the first to uncover the secret buried deep in Acadian Canada.

"Discovered in 1795 by three local teens, it is the longest-running, the most expensive, and the deadliest treasure hunt in history.

"Believed to hold buried pirate treasure, Shakespeare's original works or even the Holy Grail, it has captivated imaginations for over two hundred years.

To date, no treasure has ever been found, only an ingeniously booby-trapped shaft.

"Legend says the island will not give up its secret until seven people have died, and all the oak trees are gone. To date, six people have lost their lives and only one of the original oaks still stands.

"The Oak Island Tourism Society hopes the governments of Canada or Nova Scotia purchase the island, but it seems they are wary of becoming the next victim of the infamous Money Pit."

Elisabeth snorted. "Very interesting, Dad."

"What do you think? How much have you got saved in that piggy bank of yours? We could have our very own treasure island. Actually…" Dad took another sip of coffee. "Speaking of money, if you're interested, I may have an afterschool job lined up for you. There's this elderly woman, Mrs. Waters, and she's looking for a young student to make her…"

Elisabeth's mind drifted to Dad's stories about the Oak Island Money Pit. It was a ten-minute car ride from her house, only it wasn't an island anymore. In 1965, even before her parents were born, a causeway was built, connecting the island to the mainland with a road.

"So what do you say? Are you interested?"

Elisabeth looked up, frowning. "Huh?"

"You didn't hear a word I said about Mrs. Waters, did you?"

"Sorry, I was daydreaming."

"It's fine. I'll tell you later."

****

Arms crossed behind her head, Elisabeth was sprawled out on the second-floor staircase landing, staring off into space.

"Elisabeth?" Malcolm said with a bark of laughter as he headed down the stairs.

She jerked her head up. "Yeah?"

"You all right, lass?"

"Yes," she said, sitting up. "I'm just waiting for Quinton to be done studying. Fee's got chores to do, too."

He tilted his head to the side. "Would you like to accompany me to the village? I'm on my way now."

"Really?" She bounced onto her tiptoes. "I'd love to."

"Good. Let's go."

Smiling, she walked beside him to the stable.

"Joseph, we're going to need Dandy as well."

"Aye, sir," the skinny man said before disappearing into a stall.

A few minutes later, two horses were ready. Malcolm helped Elisabeth mount Dandy and then handed her the reins.

She cleared her throat. "I actually don't know how to steer this thing."

"This *thing*?" he said with a smirk while stroking the chestnut horse. "You've never learned to ride, have you? Dinnae fret. Dandy will just follow along. If you want to turn left, pull his reins left. If you want to turn right, pull his reins to the right. If you want to stop, pull back on them. Let him know you're the boss and you'll be fine. Just give him a little kick in the side with your heels to get him moving."

Dandy obediently followed Malcolm's huge black horse, and before long, Elisabeth felt comfortable in the saddle. They rode along a sunbaked road in relative silence. As the warm wind blew through her hair, she leaned forward, scratching Dandy's neck.

When they eventually came upon a small town, Malcolm stopped, dismounting in front of a row of half-timber buildings. The aroma of baking bread drifted out of an open window, causing Elisabeth's tummy to rumble.

"I have a business matter that needs attention. Wait right here and when I'm done, you and I will have a nice meal. I should only be a few minutes."

Elisabeth replied with a crisp nod and dismounted Dandy.

While showering the horse with loving pats, she glanced up and down the street, watching townsfolk come and go along the uneven dirt road. A mangy dog wagged its tail submissively in a doorway. A moment later, a bone was tossed outside for it. The pup grabbed it into its jaws and then pranced proudly away.

"Well, that's taken care of," Malcolm said with a sigh when he returned. "Follow me, lass. I know a place where we can get a good meal."

Elisabeth followed him a few doors down to a tavern. Inside, the dark pub smelled of yeasty beer and body odor. They walked to a table in the back, past laughing and talking patrons. Malcolm dragged a chair out for Elisabeth before cramming into a seat across from her. She ran her fingers along the crude table, watching as an older gentleman, with a big mustache, made his way over.

"Good to see you, Laird Craig," the man said, grabbing Malcolm's shoulder and holding it.

"You as well, Mr. Brown," he replied with a deep, satisfied breath. "You as well."

A slow smile built as he turned to Elisabeth. "And

who's this lovely lass?"

"This is my young ward, Elisabeth."

Mr. Brown nodded and leaned in. After inspecting her for a moment, he turned his attention back to Malcolm, this time squinting in amusement. "So, when are you going to finally settle down? Have a wife and bairns of your own?"

"When I find the right woman," he replied with a laugh too loud before changing the subject. "I'm starving. I'll have the usual. Bring a plate for the child, too."

"Aye. Right away, sir," Mr. Brown said before disappearing behind a door into the kitchen.

Malcolm shifted in his chair. "I'm sorry to tell you, lass, but we've not been able to locate your parents yet." His forehead wrinkled. "Nor Mahone Bay, for that matter."

Elisabeth cleared her throat.

Malcolm tapped his heel. "I think it's time you tell me how you ended up on my land."

She felt the color drain from her face.

Elisabeth knew the how, but not the why.

Why Scotland?

Why Castle Ealasaid?

Why the seventeenth century?

"I…um…" Elisabeth's breath burst in and out. "I was, um…" Her heartbeat raced, ready to explode.

Suddenly, Malcolm gave a sympathetic nod. "It's fine, lass," he said with a heavy sigh. "You'll tell me when you're ready."

Elisabeth swallowed and nodded.

"You know…" He leaned forward. "There has always been this mystery, and *you* seem to fit right into the middle of it."

Her eyes widened. "I do?"

"Aye. You do."

Elisabeth's posture perked up. "How?"

"Well…originally, Castle Ealasaid was a mere tower…built two hundred years ago. About sixty-five years ago, when my grandfather was the laird, he was near financial ruin. He had seventeen sisters and daughters and needed to provide for all of them."

Elisabeth gasped. "Seventeen?"

"Aye. Seventeen. One rainy evening, a weary traveler knocked on his door. My grandfather gave the stranger food and a bed for the night. The next morning, before the mysterious man left, he insisted on repaying the kindness shown to him, but my grandfather needed no payment for he was truly happy to have been in the position to help his fellow man.

"Can you imagine my grandfather's shock when he discovered the man had left behind gold? Enough gold to build Castle Ealasaid as it is today."

Elisabeth let out a spontaneous laugh.

"Now, sitting beside all the gold was a letter from the stranger asking that a beautiful castle be built so the laird's female dependents and future generations might enjoy it. His only request was that it be named after the woman he once loved and lost."

Elisabeth released an appreciative sigh. "That's so romantic."

"Coincidently…her name was *Elisabeth*."

A slow smile drifted across her face. "Are you serious?"

"Aye. Very serious."

She pressed both palms to her cheeks. "Where'd he

get all that gold? Who was his Elisabeth? How did he lose her? Did she die?"

"Nobody knows. It's always been a mystery."

Elisabeth suddenly became still. "The stranger left that much gold? Just like that? Enough to build an entire castle?"

"Aye. The man never returned, so after some time my grandfather took the gold to build the house and proudly named it *Ealasaid,* which is the Gaelic form of the name Elisabeth. We were raised to open our home for any weary traveler who ends up at our door because the entire castle was born on such an act, and we must never forget."

Elisabeth's heart felt full.

Malcolm rubbed his eyebrow. "Now…this part of the legend has to do with you, I believe."

Her posture perked up. "With me?"

"What do you make of this?" He shook his head. "The letter to my grandfather went on to say one day a child, also named Elisabeth, would be in need of our help and to, please, not turn her away."

Elisabeth's breath hitched.

"Clearly, that's you, isn't it?"

"That's…that's just plain *weird.*"

"Aye. This was way before your time, before my time too. Yet, our family's mysterious benefactor predicted your arrival." Malcolm stared down at his palms as if they held answers. "My father used to always say, 'Do not forget to entertain strangers, for by so doing some have unwittingly entertained angels.'" He looked up again, sucking in a quick breath. "And *that* is why you'll always have a home at Ealasaid, no questions asked, *Elisabeth.*"

At a loss for words, she simply shook her head. Her pulse increased wondering how someone from before the castle was even built knew she'd be coming here.

"I hope someday you'll fill in the gaps, lass, and tell—"

"Here's your supper. Be careful now, it's hot," Mr. Brown warned as he placed their food on the table.

"This looks wonderful, as usual," Malcolm said. "Dig in, lass. This is the best haggis for miles around."

"Haggis?"

"Aye. You'll love it." Malcolm's skin flushed. "It's the heart, liver, and lungs of a sheep, chopped up and mixed with onion, oatmeal, and spices, and then boiled in the lining of a sheep's stomach. Absolutely delicious."

Elisabeth let out an uncontrollable whimper as her stomach churned. Nothing like a big old plate of boiled sheep intestines to kill a healthy young appetite.

After they were done their meal, a meal Elisabeth prayed she would never have to pretend to eat again, they exited the tiny tavern and walked down the street. A stern, pompous-looking man, steering a horse-drawn covered wagon, came to a stop ahead of them.

Elisabeth's head tilted to the side, watching as the man sprang down from the driver's bench before grabbing a cane, which he clearly used as a dramatic accessory. The man had thick, overgrown eyebrows pulled tight over beady eyes, big gray sideburns stretching down his face, and his lips plastered in a perpetual frown. As he walked down the street, he held his head so high his nose seemed to stick straight into the air.

Elisabeth pulled on Malcolm's sleeve. "Who's that?"

Malcolm's jaw tightened. "I believe *that* is Robert Hobson."

She cleared her throat. "He looks like he thinks too much of himself."

He shot the man a quick glance. "Good observation," he whispered. "Hobson's a witch-hunter and prides himself on being the best in all of Scotland. He's brought countless women to trial." Malcolm shook his head. "To tell you the truth, many people don't hesitate to report suspicions of witchcraft to him."

Elisabeth twisted at her skirt while listening.

"For twenty shillings, he offers his witch-hunting services to any town or burgh willing to pay. Not only that, he charges an *additional* twenty shillings for every successful execution. So, you can be sure he searches for as many 'witches' as he can find."

She raised her eyebrows. "You don't believe in witches, do you?"

"Not I, lass, but this man sweeps into town and somehow incites folks to turn against their own neighbors and kin."

Elisabeth froze, watching as Robert Hobson entered the inn across the street.

****

The town square smelled of rotting garbage. After a crack of thunder sounded in the distance, a rat skittered down an alley. A hooded crow cawed from a nearby rooftop. The man shoved both hands into the pockets of his tattered beige jacket, watching as Jane Porter was paraded slowly through the crowd. Her skirts were filthy, her shoulders curled over her chest, and tears streamed down her cheeks. A noose hanging from the crossbeam of the wooden gallows awaited the old woman's neck.

The man's blue eyes prickled with tears, recalling events from centuries ago, when he too had been paraded through a crowd to his own execution.

He rubbed his heart, thoughts drifting back to that day in the arena—the day he first met Elisabeth.

His past.

Her future.

As young, star-crossed lovers, they'd attempted to realign the heavens themselves.

But…

Everyone knows star-crossed lovers never get happy endings.

With a deep, aching breath, the man forced his attention back to Jane Porter. A cranky old woman, Jane was known to talk to herself while working. Like many people do. She was blind in one eye so squinted with her good eye in order to see better. However, she kept to herself most of the time and went about her own business.

That was until Robert Hobson came to town.

The man heard Hobson encouraging everyone he came across to turn in suspected witches. He would be their savior, for he was here to purge their village of evil.

"Be not afraid, bring them forth."

The witch-hunter would perform his tests and bring them to trial. The guilty would be executed. The residents could then go on with their hard-working, God-fearing ways, without the devil trying to tempt them.

Names were mentioned.

Lots of names.

Accusations reached the witch-hunter's ears.

The man sat at the back of the courtroom during Jane's trial. His golden-brown hair fell onto his forehead as he stared down at his hands, fidgeting with several thin, smooth stones while listening to all the so-called evidence.

After the poor woman was arrested, she was taken to the tolbooth.

Mr. Hobson admitted he was happy to begin the witch testing.

At the trial, Hobson told how he'd searched her body for a witch's mark, which the man knew could be anything: a mole, a scar, a birthmark. Hobson testified that although he'd found nothing, he used his bodkin, a pointed, needle-like tool, to detect a spot where she didn't bleed. He'd poked her with it all over her body, ending with Jane Porter's calloused feet, which were so tough they didn't bleed. That was where, he'd exclaimed in triumph, he'd found his witch's mark.

She didn't confess though.

Hobson related to the court how he'd tied her to a chair and kept her that way for three days and three nights. She wasn't allowed to eat, sleep, or go to the bathroom in all that time. His assistants kept watch over her with strict instructions not to let any flies or bugs come near her. Insects were there to aid her, to do her work—witch's work. The men were to squish any bugs that entered the room. If one landed on her, it was proof she was a witch.

On the third day, a fly landed on her leg.

Another sign.

At her trial, although the man spoke in her defense, all her neighbors were present to testify against the old, half-blind woman.

"Jane Porter has the evil eye."

"Aye, I walked past her in town last week and she was talking to Satan himself."

"Jane made me husband get thrown from his horse when he rode past her. She did it all with her evil eye."

"All my chickens died. She put a curse on them."

Jane Porter was found guilty and sentenced to die. She would hang today, and then they'd burn her at the stake.

That was the fate of a witch.

The bloodthirsty mob, eager to watch the execution, filled the square, surrounding the man. Children laughed while adults chatted and yelled amongst themselves.

Though centuries had passed, what had changed?

Nothing.

Was this really any different from his days in the gladiatorial arena?

The man lowered his gaze, retreating from the crowd.

He had no desire to watch the old woman die.

Chapter Eleven

John stood in the doorway one summer morning, a satisfied smile on his face. During the previous year's spring, he'd cleared out some of the island's oak trees in order to build a solid, handsome house, but his wife, Sarah, had made it a home. A storey and a half tall, it was timber-framed with a clapboard exterior. Sarah insisted it be painted bright red with white trim in order to make the gray Maritime weather more bearable.

John closed his eyes and tipped his head back. It was one of those days when all seemed right with the world. "What a beautiful morning," he sang out.

"Did you say something to me, John?" Sarah called out. She was inside, feeding their baby.

"Just talking to myself," he hollered back. "See you at lunchtime."

His foolish idea to buy lot number eighteen on Oak Island wasn't so foolish after all. Now, he and his friends were once again digging their pit. This time they had the funds and the manpower to do a proper excavation.

When Simeon Lynds came to Oak Island to deliver John and Sarah's son, it was Sarah who fascinated the young doctor with the tale of buried treasure. John was well aware his wife had the gift of gab, but only his Sarah could talk a man's ear off in between contractions. Dr. Lynds was so intrigued with the mystery that he went back to Halifax, formed the Onslow Company, and raised enough money to continue searching. John, Danny, and Anthony were now hired hands, and Samuel and David often came to see how the work was progressing.

The dirt and debris, John's father had made them fill back in, were removed down to the thirty-foot level, where the three young men had left off earlier. Next, the entire structure was supported in order to avoid a possible cave-in. Each morning, candles were sent down into the pit to make sure the oxygen levels were safe. They were placed in the walls of the shaft to give off light. Everything was perfect. It wouldn't be long before little John Jr. was eating from a silver spoon.

John walked across his property. As he neared the pit, he heard Anthony's voice from deep inside it.

"What the bloody Helen…what is this? There's a layer of something down here. I don't know what it is. I'm sending a piece up. It looks like shredded tree bark."

"It's coconut fiber," David said while inspecting it. "It's used to pack fragile items on ships."

"Yep, that's definitely what it is," agreed Sam.

"Coconut trees don't grow in Nova Scotia." A slow smile spread across John's face. "It's from the West Indies, isn't it? It didn't just end up thirty-five feet below the ground, two thousand miles away on its own. Somebody put it down there."

The young men, and other men hired by the Onslow Company, dug deeper and deeper.

Forty feet, fifty feet, sixty feet…

At each ten-foot level, they continued to find oak

platforms sealed with putty.

Seventy feet, eighty feet...

The pit kept going, and so did the Onslow Company.

Danny gave a small yelp. "Whatever is down here must be worth even more than I first imagined. This is absolutely incredible."

At the ninety-foot level, they found a layer of light-colored clay.

It was hard as a brick.

Anthony attacked the clay with his pickaxe. When he was exhausted, Danny took a turn, followed by John. They eventually broke through the seal and found a large flat stone lying in the pit.

"It doesn't look like anything," Anthony grumbled as he picked it up to move it aside.

"Wait, there's something on it." John grabbed one of the candles so he could inspect it closer. "Look at the other side."

Anthony flipped it over and brushed the dirt off. The dark green stone had strange markings.

John paused to examine it. "Are those words? What do you think it says?"

"Beats me." Anthony shook his head. "Maybe it's some kind of warning, some sort of secret pirate code or something. Haul the bloody thing out and see if anyone can decipher it." He tied the rope around it before sending it up, then picked up his shovel and continued digging.

Before long, John started laughing. "I think I've got something again. There's something here."

"Probably another layer of oak." Danny pursed his lips. "Let's pack it up for the night, then. Just leave it until tomorrow."

"No. Hang on a second. Something's different." Anthony squatted to get closer. "Don't you find the dirt softer now, like mud?"

John nodded slowly. "Actually, yeah. It is." He probed the mud with a long stick. "There's something here. It feels different than an oak floor."

After crowbars were lowered, they poked them along the floor of the pit. Whatever was beneath them was large.

"I don't think it's wood. Listen." When John banged on the obstruction, it clanged, like metal. He thrust a fist into the sky. "It's got to be a vault!"

Danny sucked in a quick breath. "I can't believe we might have finally reached it. The treasure…after all this time and work—"

"And money," Anthony added with a snort.

The pit became muddier, but it also began to storm. The candles that lit the shaft flickered in the downpour.

Before leaving, John quirked an eyebrow while helping cover the pit for the night with a heavy slab of wood. "We can't do anything else right now, but it'll be fine until the morning. At least the treasure is actually within our grasp."

On the way to his house, John passed the stone with the strange markings on it. The rain washed away the dirt while he stopped to examine it again. Intrigued, he decided to bring it home for safe-keeping.

"What is it?" Sarah asked after supper.

"I don't know. It was in the pit. It's interesting, isn't it?"

She ran her fingers along the raised symbols. "I wonder what these mean."

"I'm not sure. Maybe it's some sort of warning. I don't know what to do with it. I don't think it's important, but it looks like a perfectly good piece of granite or something."

"Well..." Sarah's voice was bubbly. "I think it would look perfect over the fireplace."

John chuckled. "Really?"

"Yes," she said, wide-eyed. "How long have I been bugging you to make a mantle? You could put it front and center. It's the perfect size, and think of what a conversation piece it would be, John. Found right here on our own land."

"All right," he said, pulling her into a side hug and kissing her head. "I can do that for you."

****

"Do you know where Fee is?" Elisabeth asked Quinton after finding him down at the loch.

"Home. She's not done her chores yet."

Elisabeth's brow furrowed, watching as he used a stick to hit rocks into the water. "What are you doing?"

"Isn't it obvious?" he said with a smirk.

"You're hitting stones with a stick."

"Aye."

"That looks boring."

"It's not." Quinton picked up another stone, tossed it in the air, and then whacked it. He then grabbed Elisabeth's arm, pulling her to a run. "Come on. I've got an idea."

The two of them ran back along the path through the trees, into the walled garden, out onto the courtyard, and then down the lane, heading toward the stables.

"Where are we going?" she shouted, struggling to catch her breath.

"To the henhouse. I'll race you," he hollered as he took off even faster.

Elisabeth hiked up her skirts and was in full pursuit.

A few minutes later, they arrived at the coop, out of breath. Inside smelled like hay and manure as chickens clucked and scratched at the ground.

Quinton reached into a nesting box. "Hold your apron out so I can put these eggs in there."

Elisabeth stood beside him while he placed as many eggs as he could into her makeshift basket.

"Jonnet's going to kill us for taking them all," he said with a belly laugh.

With her apron held out, they walked carefully, all the way back to the loch.

"Put the eggs down. Then, toss them to me, one at a time. I want to see if I can hit them with the stick."

Elisabeth let out a theatrical groan. "I'm not your servant. Help me put the eggs down first and I'm playing too."

Quinton's ears turned red and he shuffled over to help. When they were finished, he stood with the stick in his hands, ready to swing.

Elisabeth held an egg in her palm, about to pitch it at him. All of a sudden, she backed away with a shudder. "Wait a minute…this is too much like a game we play at school and I hate it. It's called baseball."

Quinton's eyes widened. "You get to whack eggs with sticks at school?"

"No," she said with a snort. "We hit a ball with a wooden bat and I *suck* at it."

He scratched the back of his neck. "Oh, come on now. Throw the egg at me."

"Fine. I'll throw the egg at you." Aiming for Quinton's chest, Elisabeth whipped it at him, but he jumped back and still managed to hit it with the stick.

It splattered everywhere and they both doubled over in a fit of laughter, eggshells and messy yolk flying everywhere.

Elisabeth gasped for air. "That was hilarious."

"Your turn," Quinton said.

Her smile wavered. "Nope. Changed my mind. I'm good."

"Oh come on, it'll be fun. Just smash the egg."

Her brows pulled in, telling herself it wasn't baseball.

It might be fun to try.

After she took the stick from Quinton, he planted his feet in a wide stance, ready to toss the egg.

Elisabeth's tummy quivered as she held the stick up.

"No, dinnae stand like that," Quinton said, moving into her personal space. "You'll never hit it. Put your hands up here by your ears, not way down there."

Elisabeth raised her arms.

"Good, but hold your elbows out. You'll be able to swing the stick better. It's kind of like when I learned to use my sword."

She gave him a curt nod. "Like this?"

"Aye. Are you ready?"

"Yep."

Quinton stepped back and tossed the egg.

Elisabeth swung, but missed and had to jump back to avoid being splashed with egg goop. Her chest hitched. "I told you I'm terrible at this game. Everyone at school teases me because I'm so bad at it."

"No, you're not bad. You just need some more practice. Next time when the egg comes at you, step forward a wee bit. Try and whack it with the stick while it's still out in front of you. You dinnae want to get splattered with yolk."

Elisabeth gently bit her lip.

"Ready?"

"Yep. Go."

Quinton tossed the egg.

Hands up, elbows out, step forward, swing while it's in front...

Elisabeth whacked the egg.

Quinton bounced from foot to foot. "I told you you'd get this! Did you see that? Yolk went flying everywhere...my turn now."

They took turns smashing eggs until Elisabeth got the hang of it. When they ran out of eggs, they went looking for other things they could use. A ball seemed so boring now: apples, pears, onions, cabbages, and the messier the better.

"I'll go home and see what I can find," Elisabeth said while giving Quinton a good-natured shove.

Within moments, she held a large bag from her mother's kitchen. "These are the nastiest, most disgusting vegetables you will ever taste, Quinton."

He scrunched his nose up. "What are they?"

"Brussel sprouts. My mother used to tell me they were fairy cabbages to try and get me to eat them."

Quinton laughed. "They do look like miniature cabbages, don't they?"

"Yes, but..." She dissolved into a fit of giggles. "This is what *should* be done to them."

For the next several days, all three children played

this new game.

Quinton's head tilted to the side. "What's the name of this again?"

Elisabeth scrunched her nose up. "Baseball. But it's not quite the same. And besides, I hate baseball, so let's give this a different name because this is fun."

"What should we call it then?" he asked.

"How about…Splatterball?" Fiona suggested.

"Brusselball?" Quinton shouted as Elisabeth tossed a brussel sprout at him.

"Haggisball!" Elisabeth squealed. "This is what *should* be done to haggis! Malcolm made me eat that stuff once."

Fiona gasped. "You don't like haggis?"

Elisabeth shot her a wide-eyed look causing them both to burst into giggles again.

Quinton clutched Fiona's arm for support. "How about Wasteball?"

"Disgusting Scottish Food Ball!" Elisabeth screamed, holding her sides from laughing so hard.

Elisabeth had the hang of it. Almost every time she played Wasteball, she could hit things with the stick. It didn't matter if it was as big as cabbage or as small as an egg. She was good at it now and couldn't wait until her next gym class at school to prove it.

Chapter Twelve

Fiona pranced into the center of the garden maze, grinning when she found Elisabeth and Quinton sprawled out on blankets and cushions they'd dragged here from inside the castle. Her eyes sparkled as she waved her arms in the air. "Guess what?"

A genuine smile built on Elisabeth's face and she looked up from her book. "What?"

"Shona said if I want to help Jonnet peel apples in the kitchen, I can take an *entire* apple pie home later today to share with my family. It shouldn't take me too long to do that."

"That's awesome." Elisabeth held up her book. "I only have a few more chapters left so I'm going to stay and finish it. If I'm not here, I'll be at the stable visiting Dandy."

"Wait…" Quinton jumped up, shoving a superhero comic book into Elisabeth's backpack. She'd bought it for him with her allowance. "I have some lessons this morning and have to go too. I'll walk out with you, Fee."

When Elisabeth shot Quinton a knowing grin, a flush crept across his cheeks and he avoided eye contact with her.

"Hurry up, then." Fiona giggled before racing through the evergreen hedges, disappearing into the maze ahead of him.

The courtyard in the middle of the labyrinth was the perfect place for privacy as none of the adults ever seemed to venture inside. Fiona and Quinton could use electronics, read books and magazines *technically* not yet written, and be safe from the prying eyes of grown-ups. To Elisabeth's seventeenth-century friends, the gadgets were nothing short of magic. She even hosted the occasional movie night, complete with popcorn and fizzy pop. The only spot of concern from prying eyes was a small section of the upper castle with windows overlooking the maze, but the children confirmed the rooms there were all but empty. The courtyard of the labyrinth had become their perfect secret hideaway.

Elisabeth buried her nose in the book again, her pulse increasing while turning the final pages. When finished, she let out a satisfied sigh, slipped it into her backpack, and hid the bag in the evergreen boughs. After folding the blankets and placing them with the cushions atop one of the benches, she wandered out of the maze.

Outside, Elisabeth locked the door and hid the key beneath the rock. Here, the walled kitchen garden, now filled with discolored and tattered leaves, overflowed with fresh produce. An empty harvest basket sat next to a shovel left thrust in the dirt. While making her way to the arched entrance, she spotted a bushel of red apples and took one, polishing it on her sleeve until it shone.

In the distance, a dog howled.

It didn't sound like Talbot.

Biting into the tart apple, Elisabeth strolled down to the stable, eager to see Dandy. She'd come to adore that sweet chestnut horse and spent a lot of time hanging around him when Quinton and Fiona were busy. It also helped that, despite his gruff exterior, Joseph no longer frightened her, either.

Elisabeth climbed up on the split rail fence, checking to see if the paddock was empty. The only grazing animal was a fat rabbit. After stepping down and wandering into the stone building, she squinted, waiting for her eyes to adjust to the darkness. A horse pawed at the ground. Another whinnied. She ran her fingers along the wall of stalls, heading straight for Dandy's.

After a door squeaked, Elisabeth couldn't shake the feeling of being watched.

Her heart raced.

Then, footsteps scuffed the ground behind her.

"Joseph?" Elisabeth called out as she turned around, attempting to keep her voice light.

Silence.

She cleared her throat, convincing herself one of the horses made the noise while continuing toward Dandy's stall.

Hay crunched underfoot.

With an uncontrollable whimper, she glanced over her shoulder just as someone lunged, grabbing her from behind. Elisabeth let out a sharp scream as they locked both arms at her sides, trying to drag her toward the tack room. With rasping breaths, she kicked and fought back, managing to twist halfway around, but unable to break free. Blinded by bright sunshine streaming in from the entrance door, it left her cloaked attacker nothing more than a shadow.

In the struggle, the hooded figure pushed her.

Hard.

Elisabeth lost her balance. She stumbled sideways, bashed her head against the wall, and then on the ground.

The assailant gasped.

After that, everything turned to darkness.

****

The air smelled of hay and dust. Agitated horses whinnied and snorted. Other's stomped their hooves. Elisabeth opened her eyes, blinking several times. Her brows squished together while staring at a half-eaten apple on the dirt floor. She sat up, groaning while rubbing two separate lumps forming on her head. The last thing she remembered was going to visit Dandy…

With a heavy feeling in her stomach, a recollection of events that transpired moments ago came flooding back. Elisabeth's hand flew to her throat, feeling for the crystal.

She shook her head in denial.

The necklace was gone.

Trembling, she searched the floor on hands and knees, until her chest caved in.

The crystal was nowhere to be found.

Using the wall for support, Elisabeth pulled herself up. Her nostrils flared realizing Quinton and Fiona were the *only* ones who knew what it was capable of.

Quinton had already messed with her once; convincing her she was going to *hang* for stealing his horse.

And what about Fiona? She may be small but had no problem tackling Quinton to the ground in the maze.

Was one of them trying to lock her in the tack room as a prank?

Hide the necklace?

Well…accidental or not, this time their stupid prank went too far. It crossed the line. Both knew how important that crystal was to her so they better not lose it in the meantime. This wasn't even *remotely* funny. Being shoved and knocked out in the process was just the icing on the cake.

Joseph mumbled to himself as he walked into the stable. When Elisabeth took a step, her head spun. She grabbed onto the wall once again for support.

"You all right, lass?" Joseph clutched her by the arm and helped her sit on a nearby hay bale.

"Yeah…I just need to rest a minute," Elisabeth muttered, still feeling woozy. "By any chance, did you…did you see Quinton or Fiona in here earlier?"

Joseph picked up a pail of feed. "They were both here, aye. Said they were looking for you."

"Thanks," she muttered.

After some time, Elisabeth rose to her feet and weaved her way drunkenly back to the castle. Her chest hitched from holding back sobs. Overwhelmed by the betrayal, she went straight to her room, unsure of how to get even with her *former* friends.

Chapter Thirteen

It was a cool morning in Atlantic Canada. Gentle waves on the bay rocked the boat as Samuel and David rowed toward Oak Island, curious to check on the progress of the treasure hunt. From the beach, they heard the commotion and ran toward it.

John was soaking wet. "Un-bloody-believable," he yelled, tucking both hands into his armpits to stay warm.

David's brow wrinkled. "Is everyone all right?"

"Yeah, everyone's fine." Anthony paced back and forth. "I just can't believe it. For every step forward, we take three back."

"I'm going home to change into something dry before I freeze to death," John said with chattering teeth. "I'll be back in a few minutes."

David's posture perked up and he sprinted to catch up. "What happened?"

John groaned as he pulled his wet shirt off. "Last night, we dug down to about ninety-three feet and discovered something metal below us. We had to stop working because of the storm, though. So, we show up to continue this morning and when they lowered me in a few minutes ago, it was into a blasted pit of water."

David frowned. "How'd the hole fill with so much rain water in the night?"

"That's the thing…" John shot him an incredulous look. "It wasn't rain water. It filled up with about sixty feet of sea water!"

"John…?" Sarah burst through the front door, their chubby, content baby attached to her hip. "What happened? Are you all right? Please tell me you're—"

John tossed the wet shirt aside and immediately reached out for his wife. "Yeah, don't worry. I'm fine," he whispered, kissing her forehead before holding their son.

Sarah exhaled a heavy sigh of relief, ushering everyone into the house. "Then go change out of those clothes before you catch your death."

"I'll be right back," John said, playfully balancing the baby's stomach on his head and holding the boy's dimpled little arms in both hands as he climbed the stairs.

David stood in the doorway, a longing gaze on his face as he listened to squeals of laughter from father and son drift down from upstairs, filling the house with the happiest noise. He stared down at his hands and took a deep breath. "It smells delicious in here, Sarah."

"Thanks." She looked up from the work table, a gleam in her eye. "I've got apples and cinnamon on the fire and these…" She paused while rolling out a ball of dough. "These will eventually be biscuits—I hope," she added, chuckling. "Last time I tried to make them they turned out more like rocks."

A slow smile built on David's face. "I'm sure they were delicious."

"No, I burnt them," she said with a snort before crouching in front of the hearth to shovel glowing embers onto the lid of a heavy pot.

David's posture then stiffened as he stared at the fireplace mantle above her head. "Did John put that up there? That's the stone from the pit, right?"

Sarah's hand rested on her growing belly for a moment after she stood up. "Yes. I asked him to. It's kind of pretty. Plus, I thought it would make an interesting conversation piece."

"Well…" David clamped his lips together, trying not to laugh. "That's *definitely* an interesting place for it."

****

John pushed his sleeves up. "I've been thinking this over, and I think there's something else we can try. As you know, no matter how much water we pump out, the water level never goes down."

The others nodded.

"Well, what if we make a brand new shaft next to the one we've been digging? We'll burrow down beside it, and go about ten feet deeper than our pit. Then, we just have to tunnel over to the original excavation and grab the treasure. That way, we'll avoid whatever's causing the flooding."

"Well, that just might work," Danny McGinnis said with a wide grin as he slapped John on the back. "It's a brilliant idea. Why don't you tell Dr. Lynds, see what he thinks? He is the money, after all."

Dr. Lynds agreed with John, and work on a second shaft began. A new hole was

dug next to the original one. After several weeks, the men reached the same depth as their first pit.

****

John wiped sweat from his brow, leaning against the side of the pit to rest for a moment. "Have you heard from Samuel or David lately?"

"Yeah…" Anthony put his shovel down and took a swig of water from his canteen. "I saw Sam a few days ago. He's busy with his farm. David's gone."

John's head jerked back. "What do you mean *gone*?"

"I don't know the details, but basically he upped and left. Said goodbye to Sam and told him to tell us goodbye as well."

John's mouth fell open. "Why didn't he say goodbye to us himself? When will he be back?"

"Sam got the feeling he wouldn't."

John lifted his chin. "You think he's on the run or something?"

"David? Nah," Anthony said with a half-hearted shrug. "He doesn't seem the type. He's quiet and keeps to himself. I can't imagine him being an outlaw or anything."

John's brows suddenly furrowed. "Shhh… Listen…. Do you hear something? Something's not right…"

Anthony put his ear closer to the wall of the pit, listening. His hands trembled. "I got a bad feeling—"

"Pull us up! Pull us up!" John screamed, gasping for air as the wall of the shaft they were digging suddenly collapsed and water rushed in.

The men were lucky to get out.

The pit not only flooded—the water rose to the same level as the original pit.

"Both these shafts must be booby-trapped." John scrubbed a hand over his face. "Soon as we reach a certain depth, they both fill with water. The question is: where's it coming from? It's like the ocean is filling it up."

Anthony paced back and forth. "Dr. Lynds and the Onslow Company are going to run out of funds at this rate."

****

From high up in her bedroom window, Elisabeth crossed her arms, watching a man mount his horse and gallop down the driveway, away from the castle. She then gritted her teeth when Quinton and Fiona reappeared. They skipped and traipsed across the courtyard, heading toward the swing, seemingly without a care in the world. Elisabeth was about to storm out of her room to confront them when a horse-drawn wagon drove slowly up the road, stopping at the front entrance.

Robert Hobson, the witch-hunter, climbed down from the driver's bench, forgetting to grab his cane. Elisabeth tilted her head, observing something she didn't notice the first time she saw him—it wasn't a comfortable carriage he drove, but a wagon that resembled a large wooden crate. On the back was a door with metal bars.

When Shona hurried outside to greet the guest, Elisabeth's eyes narrowed, watching as the woman reached into her apron pocket and handed him something. The witch-hunter took it, slipped it inside his jacket, and then marched through the open front door.

A cold chill ran up Elisabeth's spine.

Curious to see what was going on, she raced out of her room, down the hallway, and peered over the railing in time to see Hobson had already climbed the three stone steps at the entrance and stood in the main corridor. Elisabeth crouched down low, spying on him through staircase railings three floors up.

"Mr. Hobson, this is absurd," Lady McQuade said in a carefully controlled tone.

He waved a hand in dismissal. "The girl must be handed over to me at once. If she is innocent, as you proclaim, she has nothing to fear."

"I promise you, Elisabeth London is most certainly *not* a witch…"

Elisabeth's head jerked back.

"Nor is she consorting with the dark arts," Lady McQuade added through gritted teeth. "Now, you've given me a headache. I suggest you leave this house at once before I fetch the laird."

Instead of retreating, Hobson rocked back on his heels. "I'm afraid I am not leaving without Elisabeth London. It is my duty to bring her to trial."

Elisabeth's eyes widened.

Hobson pushed his shoulders back. "Are you aware a witness saw her performing an unholy ritual? Are you also aware, Lady McQuade, she *had* in her possession an item used in black magic? It is not up to you, but rather the town council and the ministers, if they so choose, to deal with her. If she is innocent, as you so boldly declare, God will be with her."

"Who…?" Lady McQuade's tone deepened. "I want to know *who* told these awful lies about a *child*."

Elisabeth's breath caught when Shona stepped forward.

Lady McQuade shuffled back a step. "Shona? You*?* You are the one who has told these ugly lies? What on earth for? Why would you say such things?"

"Because…M'lady, it's all true." Shona began

wringing her hands. "I saw her sneak outside one night to perform one of her rituals. She killed lightning bugs and then danced around the trees, making their lights glow on her face. It was obvious she was worshipping the devil. Midges follow her around as if they're a crown on her head. And that necklace she wears? I've only ever seen one other like it. On Old Widow Ferguson. Everyone from here to Aberdeen knows Bessie Ferguson's a witch, healing folks and talking to the fairies. Oh, M'lady, how can you not see it?" Shona asked with a shaky voice. "It's all true. Elisabeth turned wee Fiona's hair a ghastly shade with some potion and somehow causes spirits to do her bidding when she wants things as simple as pie. She's corrupting the other children. Think of your son." Shona then cocked her head to the side. "I dare say the devil left that girl in the glen and the laird was bewitched into bringing her here."

Lady McQuade stood perfectly still; a grave expression on her face.

Robert Hobson reached into his pocket, pulling out the small wad of brown cloth Shona had given him outside. He folded the material back. "Behold, the witch's crystal..."

Crystal?

Elisabeth gasped, realizing it was Shona she'd encountered in the stable—not Quinton or Fiona. Her hands rushed to cover her mouth. Was Shona's original plan to lock her in the tack room until the witch hunter arrived to arrest her?

Her chest caved in.

With Hobson in possession of her crystal, the situation just became a thousand times worse. Elisabeth craned her head, trying to get a better look below.

"What is this?" Hobson's tone deepened and he held up a smooth, flat stone. "Where is the scrying crystal?"

Shona gasped. "I swear…it was there…"

In the moment of chaos, Elisabeth spotted Fiona and Quinton tiptoe through the growing crowd, inching their way toward the staircase.

"It matters not," Hobson continued. "This just shows the witch has used her powers from the devil himself to reclaim it."

Elisabeth felt light-headed, watching her friends sneak up toward the first landing.

Lady McQuade moved into Hobson's personal space, distracting him from the children who were in her line of sight. "That is quite enough of your parlour tricks," she said through clenched teeth. "As long as Elisabeth London is our ward, she is under the protection of this clan. Your claims are ridiculous."

"The lass is a witch and you'll thank me once she's lost her hold on you," Shona said quietly. "You'll see her for what she really is, you will."

Lady McQuade glared at her servant. "She is naught but a child."

"That may be," Robert Hobson said while looking down his nose at her, "but even children can do the works of the devil himself. The facts speak for themselves." He turned to Shona. "Fetch the girl to me at once."

At that moment, Quinton and Fiona raced up the stairs, now hidden from the view of both Shona and Hobson.

Elisabeth crept out of her hiding spot, running

down the hallway with her friends.

Quinton's eyes were bulging. "There's a witch-hunter here to arrest you. You've been accused of being a witch."

"And Shona stole my necklace but now it's missing…" Elisabeth's voice choked with tears as they all stumbled into her room, locking the door behind them. "I have no way of getting back home." She paced back and forth, shaking her head in denial.

Fiona grabbed her arms. "Then, we have to figure out a way to get you out of here without being seen. We cannot trust *anyone*."

Quinton's brow furrowed. "The witch-hunter *will* take you to the tolbooth. I don't know how much longer Mother can hold him off."

Fiona moaned.

Elisabeth's gaze darted all over the room. She couldn't shimmy down the outside wall of the castle using sheets and blankets to escape. They were too high up. "Think, Elisabeth, think," she said, curling both arms over her head.

While staring at the carpet on the floor, a thought came to her. She pushed her shoulders back realizing that although it wasn't brilliant, it was better than nothing. "Quick…help me pull the carpet away from the furniture. I saw a movie about Cleopatra once. She was rolled up in a carpet, smuggled past enemy lines, and delivered to Caesar in the palace."

With precise movements, Quinton went straight to work, helping pull the carpet into the center of the room. "We have to hurry!"

Elisabeth lay down at one end and her two friends rolled her across the bedroom floor until she was embedded in the middle. She tilted her head up a bit to get some fresh air through the one end, whimpering as part of the carpet lifted off the floor.

She was dragged to the door.

The door creaked open.

She was tugged a little further…

The door creaked and latched shut.

"Don't make any noise," Fiona whispered. "We're going to pull you down the corridor now."

Tucked inside the rug, Elisabeth crossed her fingers and hoped her crazy idea would work.

When they eventually came to a stop, she heard Fiona gasp. "There's even more people downstairs now."

"Let me see," Quinton said before dropping the carpet, with Elisabeth inside it, onto the floor.

"Lady McQuade, do not mock the law," Hobson growled. "I will search every single room myself if I must."

Fiona's voice sounded shaky. "Quinton, the rug is so heavy. I have no idea how we are going to carry her down all these stairs, let alone past the witch-hunter and—"

"What are you bairns up to?" Malcolm's tone softened as he neared. "And what are you doing with that carpet?"

Quinton began speaking rapidly. "Shona asked Fiona to bring it outside to be cleaned and she was struggling with it and so I offered to help her, and then we—"

"Wait…Shona asked *Fiona* to carry it outside?" Malcolm cleared his throat. "Here…let me help you. It's far too heavy for *either* of you."

136

Elisabeth felt herself being swung over the laird's strong shoulder.

The movement caused dust to fly.

That, unfortunately, caused the carpet to let out a delicate little sneeze.

"Achoo."

Quinton gasped. "Bless you, Fiona," he said with a high-pitched voice.

"Achoo," Fiona faked. "Achoo! Thank you. I can't seem to stop sneezing today. A-a-a-choo."

Elisabeth heard Malcolm chuckle while adjusting the carpet on his shoulder. "For some reason, this is heavier than I expected." He smacked the rug right where Elisabeth's bottom was. "I think I'll just throw it down the stairs. That's the easiest way, don't you think?"

"NO—" her friends cried in unison.

A roar came from the mob in the hall and she could feel Malcolm lean toward the railing. "What in God's name is going on downstairs?"

"We have no idea, do we, Quinton?"

"Right. No idea," Quinton agreed. "Are you going to help us or not?"

"Aye, I'll bring it downstairs for you." Malcolm carried the carpet down the stairs and past all the people. Before they stepped outside, however, she heard Lady McQuade.

"Brother, there you are," she said, relief evident in her voice.

"Laird Craig, I am Robert Hobson, and I—"

"Just a minute everyone, just a minute. I'll be right back." Malcolm continued out the door, leaving the unsuspecting Mr. Hobson behind.

"Where do you want it?" he asked once they were outside.

"Over there," Fiona said.

Malcolm put the rug gently down and the children waited in silence a few moments until he left.

Then, they unrolled Elisabeth as fast as they could.

With a shaky laugh, she jumped up.

Quinton began pacing. "I'll go back inside and do something to cause a distraction. When the witch hunter starts looking for you, I'll lead him in another direction. That should buy you time to get safely out of here and hide."

Elisabeth held her breath. "Can I borrow Dandy?"

"Aye, of course. Dinnae worry. I'll keep the witch-hunter distracted for as long as I can." Quinton shook out his hands and then forced himself to walk naturally back into the castle.

Before Elisabeth ran to the stable, she glanced at Robert Hobson's wagon and then at Fiona. "Is it hard to detach horses from a wagon?"

"Not for me." With fluttery movements, Fiona went straight to work and before long, the horses were free.

Elisabeth looked at the door. Everyone was still yelling and hollering inside. "Follow me," she whispered.

Fiona and Elisabeth led Hobson's horses across the courtyard, into the walled garden, stopping outside of the locked door to the garden maze. Her hands shook while reaching for the key. Then, the girls entered the hedge maze, ushering the horses through the labyrinth. Around each tall row of green shrubberies, the horses clomped along, finally arriving in the center of the maze.

Fiona stroked one of the horse's neck. "Let's see how long it takes him to find you in here, and then let's see him try to get you out. That ought to give us a good head start, don't you think so?"

"Us?" Elisabeth retrieved her backpack from the bushes and swung it over her shoulder. "No, Fiona. You don't want this kind of trouble."

"Look, I'm coming with you. Besides, you don't even know how to harness Dandy. Meet me at the same place we rode him the first day and we'll get out of—"

At that moment, someone tapped at a window overhead, from within one of the empty rooms overlooking the maze.

Elisabeth held her stomach while looking up.

When she saw Quinton laughing and pointing at the horses, she let out a sigh of relief.

He then motioned for her to go.

She nodded and waved goodbye, running out of the maze with Fiona.

When they reached the lane, they split up. Fiona raced to the stable, Elisabeth through the meadow to the edge of the forest.

She crouched down low not to be seen by anyone, finally letting out a huge breath when Dandy came galloping toward her.

She climbed up on the tree stump, waiting…

When Fiona slowed the horse, Elisabeth reached up, grabbed the pommel, and pulled. Her mounting wasn't graceful. She was caught up in a tangle of skirts, and half hung off the back of the saddle, but she held on and managed to straighten herself out. Fiona then clucked to the horse, and they galloped off as fast as

Dandy would take them.

Elisabeth glanced around uneasily. "You shouldn't have come with me, Fee—"

"Don't be absurd. Of course I'm coming with you. We're kindred spirits."

Her chin started to tremble. "Any idea where we should go?"

"I'm not sure." Fiona shook her head. "But as far away from here as we can get seems like the best plan...for now anyway."

As the girls pressed on through the forest surrounding Ealasaid, Elisabeth continually looked behind to make sure no one was in pursuit.

Eventually, they stopped next to a shallow stream so Dandy could rest. They'd left the woods and were now in rolling hills carpeted with purple heather, its woodsy scent filling the air. The rocks and boulders dotting the landscape reminded Elisabeth of when she'd first arrived here in Scotland. As Dandy drank, the girls gulped mouthfuls of water from their cupped hands.

Scrubby bushes caught on Elisabeth's skirt when she made her way toward a short tree. With a worried sigh, she flopped down beneath it. "What am I going to do?"

"We'll think of something," Fiona said in a soothing tone.

"Hey..." Elisabeth held her breath. "Shona said someone has a crystal like mine and everyone—"

"Aye! Old Widow Ferguson has one like it and people come from all around to see her. Most of the priests don't like her, but they leave her be because she's cured an awful lot of people with her magic water and won't take a single shilling. I've never seen her before, so I don't know much else about her." Fiona leaned in. "I think she may be the best person to help you…the only problem is I don't know where she lives. Somewhere near Stonehaven, but that's really all I know."

Determination and fear spurred Elizabeth forward. "We should go and look for her."

"Definitely." As Fiona stood up and glanced around, the wind whistled through the heather. She frowned and pointed to the winding dirt path they'd been following. "I *think* if we keep heading the way we were, it'll take us into Stonehaven."

After mounting Dandy, the girls continued in search of Old Widow Ferguson. Eventually, the weather started to turn. Low, dark clouds loomed over them and cool air blew into their faces. But, they continued for what felt like hours, following the path as it twisted into a dark forest.

Elisabeth's brow wrinkled as she looked around.

Dandy neighed, obviously spooked by something.

Then…the *something* growled.

Elisabeth felt the colour drain from her face, and she wrapped her arms around Fiona tighter.

"Go! Go, Dandy!" Fiona said with a shrill voice. "Come on…come on…"

As Dandy galloped at full speed, Elisabeth spotted a huge black dog running alongside them, stalking them from the trees.

The relentless dog, foaming at the mouth, somehow managed to keep up.

When it finally ran off in another direction, Elisabeth let out a slight moan. "I think it's gone. What should we—"

They rounded a corner and Dandy suddenly neighed. The horse reared up in terror, thrashing his front legs in the air. As Fiona struggled to keep hold of the reins, Elisabeth was thrown from the saddle.

When she hit the ground, she froze...staring into morbid yellow eyes.

The creature seemed more beast than dog. Its back arched while baring enormous fangs.

As the dog's mouth dripped with foam and the fresh blood of a recent kill, Elisabeth's eyes widened.

Rabies.

The possessed-looking dog stalked toward them, a low growl coming from its throat. One step at a time, it drew closer and closer.

Ignoring Fiona and Dandy, it crept toward Elisabeth as she cowered on the ground.

She noticed a long stick and, moving as slowly as possible, tried to reach for it.

When the dog took another step, the horse whinnied and pinned his ears back. The whites of Dandy's eyes were enormous as he stamped his feet while Fiona struggled to keep him under control.

Elisabeth gasped for air, about to grab the stick when Fiona let out a primal scream as Dandy bolted.

"Elisabeth...dinnae move!" Malcolm suddenly shouted.

She gasped as his dagger flew past her head, whirling through the air, and tearing into the flesh of the mad dog. Her posture slumped when it howled a death roar and took off, fleeing into the trees and out of view.

Malcolm then turned his attention to Fiona, who was struggling to stay atop Dandy. He caught up to the panicked horse, rode alongside, and managed to grab the reins, pulling Dandy's head back, making him run in circles until he calmed down.

"Shhhh, that's a good boy," he crooned while leading them back to where Elisabeth remained huddled on the ground, trembling.

Malcolm's tone deepened as he dismounted. "Are you lasses *trying* to get yourselves killed?" His nostrils were flaring. "Do you know how close you were to being that bloody devil's meal?"

When Elisabeth let out an uncontrollable sob, Malcolm walked closer. He then let out a huge breath. "My God, that was a close call. Are you all right?"

Elisabeth's eyes barely lifted to look at him as she stood and nodded. She struggled to hold back tears. Malcolm hugged her, reminding her immediately of her dad.

"There, there, lass. It's all right now."

Still atop Dandy, Fiona gave him an incredulous look. "How did you know we were here?"

Malcolm's brow lifted as he looked at her. "Because I've been tracking you *galoots* from the moment I discovered what the ruckus at home was about. I am absolutely furious with both of you. Do you know how dangerous it is out here? You're two wee lasses on nothing more than a pony, for bloody sake. I swear…" Malcolm then slanted his body away from them and paced back and forth. He ran his hands through his hair, clearly trying to control his temper. When he turned back to Elisabeth, he scraped a hand over his face. "I knew you were wrapped in the carpet but didn't think it was more than a silly game. I didn't want you foolish bairns getting hurt falling down the staircase." He paused, taking a deep breath. "I had *no* idea that vile man had come to arrest you on those ridiculous charges."

"Shona's the one who started it," Elisabeth said with an emotion-choked voice as she moved closer to him.

"I know…" The laird's tone became soothing. "My sister told me everything. Believe me, I will deal with Shona when I return. *You* shouldn't have run off, though. I wouldn't have let him take you. He would have had to get past me first." Malcolm then lifted Elisabeth onto the saddle of his horse before mounting behind her.

Fiona placed a hand over her heart. "You've been tracking us the entire time?"

"Aye, Fiona."

She released an appreciative sigh. "I had no idea."

"What I haven't been able to figure out is where you're running off to. Did you even *have* a plan?"

Fiona pushed her shoulders back while adjusting Dandy's reins. "Stonehaven. I was bringing Elisabeth to Stonehaven."

Malcolm shook his head. "You're not even heading in the right direction. I'll take you to Stonehaven, but only because poor Dandy here will never make the trip back carrying you two fools. Your father should still be there, Fiona, so he can bring you both home in his wagon."

With Malcolm now leading the way, they changed course and after a time, Elisabeth saw a little harbour town in the distance.

Chapter Fourteen

Even in early autumn, the horseback ride to the seaside village of Kinneff tended to be a chilly one. The man pulled his jacket tighter as wind off the North Sea picked up. A bold rabbit joined him along the narrow footpath lining the cliff edge; both sides flanked with waist-high grasses and dotted with the dainty white wildflowers Elisabeth had called Queen Anne's lace.

He stopped and dismounted, letting his horse rest while gazing out over Strathlethan Bay and along the wild coastline. Serenaded by countless birds, he listened to waves crashing into the shore below. To his left was the harbour town of Stonehaven. To his right was Dunnottar Castle, sitting high atop its rocky perch.

When the rabbit hopped back into the wildflowers next to the path, the man turned to watch it go. He then led his horse the short distance to Bessie Ferguson's thatched-roof cottage. The whitewashed house sat nestled into the landscape, enclosed by a drystone fence. A front door painted deep red matched three evenly spaced red window frames. As always, her gate was wide open and people lined up, hoping desperately for a miracle.

With a slight smile, he thought about her "healing abilities" and how everyone came to seek help from

Bessie and her crystal. She'd convinced them it was a gift from the Fairies.

From listening to conversations in town, the man was relieved to learn most of her neighbors had made up their minds she wasn't a witch, for all of her works were good. It was also said the well behind her house had healing powers. If you took a sip of its water, with her permission, of course, it could cure your sickness.

The man thought it ironic how superstitions ran wild here, yet it was so easy to be accused of witchcraft.

Because Bessie was a healer, the townsfolk accepted her...and no witch-hunters had ventured this far north, yet.

As the man walked closer, his eyes prickled with tears. Wanting to remain separate from the crowd lining the stone fence, he leaned against a shady tree to wait. He hadn't seen Bessie in years, but she'd recognize him.

She stood outside her front door, next to a nervous-looking young woman with a baby in her arms. Bessie squeezed the woman's shoulder and handed the mother a vial of her healing water. "Give some of this to your son and he'll be better within hours."

The woman's posture slumped in relief. She thanked Bessie and gave her a basket filled with goods in appreciation.

Old Widow Ferguson could have been one of the richest women in the Highlands had she accepted money, for everyone came to visit her, from the wealthiest merchants to the lowliest beggars. Bessie wanted no part of profiting from her "gift". She took only what she needed to survive and gave the rest away.

Bessie could have had her fields filled with cattle and every variety of livestock. She could have lived in a grand home and had bags filled with coins, but instead, she lived a simple, yet comfortable, life.

As the man had insisted.

The young mother hurried away, clasping the bottle of Bessie's water in her hands.

"Mrs. Bessie, I need yer help. All my cattle are dying. The bloody lot of them. If they die, my family and I will lose everything. Those cattle are our only means of survival, our only source of income. Please, can you help us?" begged a frazzled farmer next in line to see her.

Still leaning against the tree, the man rubbed an eyebrow as he watched Bessie and the farmer. He clamped his lips together to keep from laughing when Bessie gazed into her crystal. She could be so melodramatic.

"You silly fool," she said with a grim twist to her mouth. "You've made your wife happy, but have angered the Fae. You planted a rosebush for your wife along a fairy path. As soon as you move it, your cattle will be fine. You've just vexed the Fairies, is all. Before you do that, give each of your cattle a wee bit of my healing water."

The farmer thanked her, paid by way of gifts, and then hurried away, no doubt to return home and move his wife's rosebush to a different spot.

The man found it amusing that, contrary to her nickname, Old Widow Ferguson was not old. Barely thirty years old, Bessie was an attractive, robust woman with blonde hair, blue eyes, and an ivory complexion. Born outside of Inverness, she had been a shy little girl who liked to sit by herself rather than play with other children. She told her mother she could see the "wee folk," the fairies, and her mother listened to all of Bessie's fanciful tales.

As an acquaintance of her father, the man was actually the one who had gifted Bessie the crystal when she was a young girl. In reality, it was nothing more than a simple glass jewel he'd crafted himself that she'd taken a fancy to.

When she was eight years old, both parents died within days of each other, leaving Bessie orphaned and alone in the world. She begged on the streets to survive until the man found out and convinced a kind old doctor to take pity on the small child and keep her as a young servant girl.

She was a bright child and learned about herbs and medicine in the years she watched the doctor care for his patients. Most medicines were made from local plants, and young Bessie would be sent to gather the leaves and berries for him to use in his concoctions. He died when she was twelve years old, and she was once again left to her own devices to fight for her survival.

The man's chest tightened, regretting he hadn't been there to intervene on her behalf the second time.

Seven long years after the doctor's death, she arrived in Stonehaven. Standing in the pouring rain, bewildered and lost, with the glass jewel clasped in her hands. The man's head jerked back when Bessie approached him on the street.

She'd recognized him immediately, of course.

In desperate need of food and shelter, he introduced her to an older man named Duncan Ferguson. Duncan took an immediate liking to her. He was a local fisherman and because he could provide a stable home for her, she agreed to marry him. He was a kind and gentle man and through their years of marriage, she grew to care for him.

Bessie never spoke to the locals of those seven years prior to her arrival in Stonehaven. She enjoyed the mysteriousness. Many people convinced themselves she'd gone to live with the Fairy Folk during that time, learned their magic, and received her infamous crystal from them. It was all speculation, of course, because she never revealed the truth of her "magic" to anyone, not even to her husband when he was alive.

The man, however, knew the truth.

The *real* healing magic was from another source.

As Bessie looked beyond the line of people waiting to see her, he tipped his head to catch her attention. When their eyes locked, her mouth fell open.

"I'm terribly sorry everyone. It's late. The rest of you will have to come back in the morrow," she said, shooing those still waiting away. She then rushed toward the man with arms outstretched, a crooked smile on her face. "I hardly recognized you."

"Very funny," he said with a snort.

Bessie let out an appreciative sigh and pulled him into a hug. "You always stay away far too long, David."

His smile quivered when he pulled back. "She's here."

Bessie gasped. "Elisabeth? Well…" She smoothed down her skirt. "You already know I'll take good care of her."

His shoulders dropped. "I know."

"You know what else?" She leaned closer, squeezing his arm. "One day, all that torment etched in those blue eyes of yours is going to be gone. You'll see. You've come this far, haven't you?"

David's chest hitched and he brought a shaky hand to his forehead. "I'm trying. God knows I'm trying."

"Don't look so worried," Bessie said with a steady, lower-pitched voice. "I'll prepare her room, grab my shawl and a lantern, and then go find her."

"Do you remember what to tell her?"

"I'd have no *honour* if I forgot, now would I?" she said with a wide smile.

He turned away to hide a grin. "I can see why you two got along. You've the same *ridiculous* sense of humor." His eyebrows then drew together. "She's only twelve right now and doesn't know me yet. She's going to be terrified and all alone."

Bessie nodded in understanding.

"She's..." He cleared his throat while holding out his hand. A simple bracelet of rope and red ribbon, beautifully entwined together, sat in his palm. "She's wearing this red string in her hair."

Bessie's hand covered her mouth. "Is that...? Is that the knot you—?"

"Yes," he muttered before stashing the sentimental item safely away again. "Before we were sold."

"David Perrier..." she said in a soothing tone. "Will you stop worrying so much? I've got this."

He closed his eyes and nodded. "Thank you."

****

As Fiona, Elisabeth and Malcolm rode into Stonehaven, the already dark gray sky threatened to spill over at any moment. Malcolm led them down the main road, beyond rows of houses and shops, toward the market square.

"Laird Craig..." a large, blond-haired man called out with a bark of laughter and jogged toward them. "You certainly got here fast. I take it you got the message?"

Malcolm's eyes narrowed. "What message?"

The man's head jerked back. "You haven't heard?"

"No, I haven't. I'm here on other matters. Family matters."

He shook his head. "Well, lucky you're here now."

"Excuse me a moment," Malcolm said as he dismounted his horse, and walked a few steps away with the man.

They spoke in low voices. The blond-haired man was gesturing with his hands and Malcolm was shaking his head.

Malcolm's fists tightened. "All right, I'll see you in a few minutes," he said, walking back toward the girls. "I have to deal with these two first."

Malcolm led both horses into the market square where they found Fiona's father preparing his wagon for the trip home.

Mr. McAllistair gasped as his daughter dismounted Dandy. "Fiona? What in God's name are ye doing here, lass?" He then held his stomach as if in pain when noticing Malcolm. "Laird Craig? Oh dear God...is...is everythin' all right at home?"

"Aye, Mr. McAllistair, I assure you, everyone at home is fine," Malcolm said with a polite smile. "Would you be so kind as to deliver my ward, Elisabeth, to Castle Ealasaid on your return home? Dandy as well. I'll let *them* explain the details to you."

"Aye, aye," he said in a confused tone. "Of course, Laird Craig, sir."

"Very well. I leave them in your capable hands as I have some urgent matters that need my attention."

Malcolm lifted Elisabeth down. After tipping his head at Fiona's father, he mounted his horse, which then trotted away.

Mr. McAllistair's brows squished together when he turned to Fiona, "You'd best have a good explanation, young lady."

Elisabeth bit her lip realizing she had a problem.

She couldn't return to the castle. Not now. She had to find Bessie Ferguson first. What if there was some way the woman could help her return home? Home to the future?

As Mr. McAllistair prepared his horse and wagon for the return trip, Fiona explained the best she could about the circumstances that led to their great escape earlier.

Her father listened as he worked, not saying a word.

Elisabeth stood nearby, silent, trying to remain as invisible as possible. As she listened, her chest tightened. This was all her fault. Fiona wouldn't be in this mess without her.

"But, Papa—"

"Fee, I said no. Who am I to disobey an order from the laird?"

Fiona clasped both hands under her chin. "*Please*, you *have* to bring us to Old Widow Ferguson—"

"Old Widow Ferguson?" He scratched at his cheek. "Is something ailing Elisabeth?"

"No."

"Then that's the *last* place she should go if a witch hunter's trying to arrest her."

Elisabeth's muscles tightened knowing she had no choice. She had to find Bessie Ferguson on her own. She should leave before ruining Fiona's life any further. What if the witch-hunter found her and arrested Fiona, as well as Elisabeth, because of their association?

She bit down on her nails, unable to bear the thought of anything bad happening to her friend. Fiona was already in enough trouble and Elisabeth could no longer drag her through this mess. She needed to go back to her regular life, hiding from chores under trees with Quinton. Elisabeth would miss them all, but she needed to find her own way home.

She eyed an alley nearby, adjusted her backpack, and then took several steps backward, unnoticed by both father and daughter.

Her heart raced, waiting for the opportunity.

When they both glanced away for a moment, she slipped behind a wall and then fled down a dirt road without looking back. Her chest hitched while running along the small corridors of the town, looking for a spot to hide. Elisabeth's vision clouded with tears, realizing for the first time who she'd miss most of all.

She stopped, leaning over with both hands on her knees.

While thinking about how disappointed Malcolm would be, Elisabeth let out an uncontrollable sob.

****

With manic energy, Elisabeth wandered up and down dark streets for what seemed like hours. She didn't know if Fiona and her father were looking for her, or if they had left. The sun had set and rain began to fall. Elisabeth trembled, now unsure she'd made the right decision.

A window opened above her. "Gardyloo!" a woman shouted before throwing something out the window.

The contents splashed onto the ground, just missing Elisabeth as it splattered everywhere. She recoiled at the horrible stench; quickly figuring out it was the contents of a chamber pot being washed away by the rain.

What she wouldn't give for a hot shower right now, a proper toilet, comfy pajamas...and to be home. Her eyes clouded with tears. How was she going to find Bessie Ferguson when no one was out in this rain? Once she found her way to Bessie's door, she'd beg, on hands and knees if necessary, until the woman helped.

Elisabeth jumped as lightning cracked. She shivered in her wet clothing and when tiny droplets of water fell from the tip of her nose, she wasn't sure if they were raindrops or teardrops. Exhausted, she eventually crumpled onto the ground in the street, holing up in the doorway of a shop closed for the night. She pulled both knees up to her chest and tried to control her difficult breathing.

"Hey there, lassie..." *Hiccup.* "Yer not crying, are ye?"

Elisabeth's head jerked back when a greasy-looking man grabbed her arm, roughly yanking her up while ogling her. He smelled like smoke and alcohol. Elisabeth's heart pounded. As he wobbled on his feet, she kicked him in the shins, broke free from his grasp, and scurried away, fast.

"Hey. Where you goin'? I was jist asking you a question is all." *Hiccup.* "And why'd ye kick me?" he added with a moan.

She wandered the streets for hours.

The only people out this time of night were the type parents warned about. They were dirty, drunk, loud—

The hair lifted on Elisabeth's neck when she heard footsteps quicken behind her. Had the creep found her again? Her breath burst in and out as she picked up the pace.

"Elisabeth!" a woman's raspy voice called out. "There you are, lass." She let out a loud sigh of relief. "I've been looking everywhere for you."

Elisabeth's eyes narrowed in confusion and she spun around.

A gorgeous blonde woman held a lantern up. "Let's go. Unless you *want* to spend the whole night in the rain," she added, a playful smile on her lips.

Elisabeth froze, tilting her head to the side as the woman walked closer.

"I don't like to turn away any weary traveler who's come a long way to find me, and you've certainly come a very long way, haven't you?"

"Wait..." Elisabeth said in an uncertain tone. "*I've* been looking for *you*?"

"Aye." She leaned forward and chuckled. "I'm Old Widow Ferguson, but you can call me Bessie."

Elisabeth's mouth fell open.

"And I'm thinking you probably have a lot of questions for me," Bessie said, wrapping her shawl around Elisabeth's shoulders before pulling her into a side hug. "Come on. As soon as we get back home, you'll find a hot meal and a warm bed."

Elisabeth let out a huge breath, more than willing to follow Bessie all the way home.

Chapter Fifteen

"My dear, Sarah..." John let out a shallow sigh as he rolled peas around with his fork. "Where have the years gone?"

"I don't know," she replied, tears filling her eyes as she scooped more potatoes onto his plate. "We must have blinked." She slowly leaned back in the wooden chair. "Seems like it was only yesterday we moved to Oak Island. Now all twelve of our children are grown."

His eyes sparkled as he looked up at her. "We're grandparents though. I do like *that* part of growing older."

As they sat in comfortable silence, John's posture relaxed. He ate his meal while allowing his mind to wander back to days gone by. Although David Perrier never returned to the area, his other friends had remained. Dan McInnis moved onto Oak Island, as did Samuel Ball. Anthony Vaughan lived on the mainland, his home across from the island. They farmed the land and raised their families, but the men's true passion was finding what was buried in the pit.

Too old now to do the physical labor, they never gave up. Over time, various groups of investors tried to access the treasure and John was hopeful the Truro Company, now financing the hunt, would discover what was buried on his land.

****

Sarah's head jerked back. "What do you mean the beach is artificial?"

John paced back and forth, unable to keep still. "I was just over at the pit, talking to some of the men from the Truro Company, and…" He looked at her with a wide grin. "Oh, Sarah, this is incredible. They say the beach is fake, phony! It's hiding a brilliant drainage system."

Her eyes narrowed. "How on earth can a beach be fake?"

John reminded Sarah of what little Henry had discovered one afternoon, a few months back.

"Papa, come here."

A slow smile built as he walked over to where his grandson was playing along the rocky waterfront. "What is it, son?"

The boy's nose wrinkled. "Why is the water doing that?"

John tipped his head to the side. It was low tide and what he saw left him speechless. Water was pouring *out* of the beach.

John had then rushed to where workers were digging, and told them of the discovery. Now he said to Sarah, "So, Truro dug up the shoreline to see if there was an inlet there. What they discovered is that whoever built the pit also dug tunnels under the beach. Five of them. They lined them with rocks, coconut fiber, and eel grass so the dirt and sand were trapped by the rocks, but the water can still flow in easily."

Sarah tugged at her ear. "What on earth for?"

"Well, it turns out all the tunnels meet inland,

about five hundred feet away." John was talking quickly, waving his arms with grand gestures. "They lead to yet another tunnel. This one slopes down...and flows right into the pit. So when you dig to a certain level, you've sprung the trap and, *whoosh*, all the water from the sea comes rushing in."

Sarah stared at him, a blank look on her face. "Huh?"

John turned away and burst into laughter before walking to the fireplace. "Let's see if I can make this easier." He placed his outstretched fingers on the edge of the mantle. "See my fingers? Think of each one as a tunnel."

"Okay. I'm with you so far," Sarah said.

"My fingers are the tunnels running under the beach. The sea flows through them and into another tunnel, represented by my forearm here, which leads to the pit. So, when you dig down to the depth of the tunnel, you open the pit to the tunnel thus springing the trap and causing the pit to flood."

Sarah's posture perked up. "But why did the second shaft flood?"

"Because we got too close to the original pit. When we tried to tunnel over to it, the pressure from the water caused the wall between the two excavations to collapse."

"My Lord, that's ingenious," Sarah said with a bark of laughter. "That's why you could never pump the water out of it. The ocean really was filling it up. So, now what?"

"Well, all they need to do is plug the tunnels and build a dam, which ought to stop the water from running into the pit. They're already talking about building a cofferdam." He whooped loudly, grabbed Sarah, and spun her around the room. "Then they go and get the treasure out!"

****

Wrapped in the shawl Bessie had given her, Elisabeth's forehead wrinkled as she followed the woman through the rain and out of town, a lantern lighting the path. They climbed a steep embankment and when Elisabeth glanced behind, she could see Stonehaven sprawled out below her. As the footpath continued upward, waves crashed against rocks and the familiar smell of salty sea air reminded her of home.

"Be careful here, lass. Watch where you step," Bessie said at one point where the ledge seemed no more than a foot away from the path.

Beneath the pale moonlight, Elisabeth bit her lip, trying to concentrate where she stepped, following Bessie along the cliff-side trail. When they reached the crest, the narrow road curved around the coastline. A short time later, she saw flames flickering in the distance. Loud voices carried on the wind.

Elisabeth paused. "What are those lights over there?"

"Soldiers' campfires at Dunnottar Castle. It's under siege by the English."

Her mouth fell open. "How long has that been going on?"

"Almost eight months." With a heavy sigh, Bessie turned down a dirt road. Elisabeth could see it led straight to the darkened cottage.

Once inside, Bessie placed the lantern on a thick windowsill next to the front door and began lighting additional candles. As they flickered and glowed,

Elisabeth dropped her backpack at the door and smiled while glancing around the space. The house had whitewashed walls, a stone floor, and appeared to be three rooms; a central kitchen and dining area, flanked by a bedroom on either side.

"I'll put the kettle on," Bessie said, arranging kindling on the ground of a large hearth situated on the right-hand side of the room. "I was given some fancy leaves that make a drink called *tea*. Comes all the way from China and let me tell you..." Her voice became high-pitched. "I've taken *quite* the fancy to it."

Elisabeth chuckled. "I can't wait to try it."

Beneath the kitchen window, a work table overflowed with baked goods. Elisabeth's nose twitched, catching the scent of warm yeasty bread. She rubbed her growling tummy while continuing to scan the cottage. Opposite the worktable was a dining table, and in the back left corner sat a hutch. Cupboard doors hid the contents at the bottom, but the upper shelves were neatly lined with cups, dishes, and an endless supply of small pots containing jams, jellies, preserves, honey, and who knows what else.

After stoking the glowing embers, Bessie hung a black kettle from a hook and placed a loaf of bread on the table.

With an unsteady walk, Elisabeth made her way to the hearth, hoping to dry her wet dress with its heat.

"Aww, you do look exhausted, poor dear." Bessie pointed to the bedroom on the left side of the house. "That'll be your room. There's a nightgown on the bed for you if you want to go change out of that soaking wet frock."

Elisabeth's eyes clouded with tears. "Yes, thank

you. Thank you for *everything*, Mrs. Ferguson," she said before stepping into the tiny room.

Bessie burst into laughter. "You're a polite little thing, aren't you? No need for formalities here, lass. Make yourself at home."

As Elisabeth undressed, a slight moan escaped while taking off her wet shoes and stockings. She slipped into a long, white nightgown that had been folded and placed atop the bed, seemingly awaiting her. The bed and a side table were the only pieces of furniture in the bedroom, but it was more than she needed. As a candle blinked on the window sill, her lips parted, noticing the bedding seemed surprisingly luxurious—almost out of place. She ran fingers along the soft fabric, longing to nestle beneath the blankets and rest her head on that pillow.

Barefoot, Elisabeth walked back into the kitchen and arranged her wet skirts on a chair near the hearth so they could dry overnight. "That bed looks *so* comfortable."

Bessie looked up from the cooking fire, her eyes twinkling with mischief as she exchanged a knowing glance with her. "He insisted you only have the best."

Elisabeth's posture stiffened. "What? Who?"

The woman confined her laughter to a snort while reaching for the kettle. "Nobody. It's nothing. Forget I said anything."

Elisabeth shifted back and forth, and then sat at the table, watching as Bessie prepared a cup of tea and placed it in front of her, followed by a bowl of stew. Her brow wrinkled. "I...I heard you have a crystal with, you know, *special powers*."

"Aye," she said, sitting and taking a sip of her tea.

"The thing is…" Elisabeth's eyes widened. "Mine was stolen from me. I need to get it back so I can go home."

"Aye, I know, child," she said in a soothing voice. "Don't fret. It'll all work out."

Elisabeth's chest caved in. "I can't help *fretting*. I need it to get back home. I'm…I'm from the future, you know," she whispered.

"Aye." Bessie took a sip of her tea. "I know."

Elisabeth's head jerked back. "Well…do you also happen to know where my crystal is?"

"No, but I know someone who does," she said with a smirk.

Elisabeth's brow furrowed and then released. "Oh, I see…I heard you supposedly talk to the *fairies*."

Bessie winked at her. "Don't tell me you don't believe in fairies and magic, lass. You, of all people."

"No…yes…" Her posture sagged. "I honestly don't know what to believe anymore." Elisabeth picked up the piece of bread Bessie had set in front of her and dipped it in the stew. "Are you trying to tell me fairies are real?" she asked in between bites.

"Well…they *used* to be real." Bessie gave a half-hearted shrug. "Most everybody here in the Highlands still believe in the wee folk, though. They'll go as far as to leave food out for the fairies at night. The Fae, in return, have been known to repay this kindness with gifts like good luck and a bountiful crop."

Elisabeth shook her head in disbelief. "What do you mean they *used* to be real?"

"Well, more than twelve thousand years ago, long before the great flood—"

"Do you mean Noah's Ark?"

"Aye, that's the flood I mean." Bessie then squinted in amusement as Elisabeth gobbled up a second piece of bread and emptied her bowl. "You want some cake, lass?"

Elisabeth's eyes widened. "Yes, please."

Bessie cut a big slice and brought it to the table. "You're certainly hungry, aren't you?"

"Starving," Elisabeth tried to say politely while placing a hand over her full mouth.

Bessie chuckled as she sat and took another sip of tea before leaning closer, continuing her story. "Long before the great flood, there was a race of people on earth. They were advanced in mathematics and science; men admired them and considered them magicians. This race was the fairies. The Fae loved beauty. They loved nature; animals, plants, and they treasured this earth of ours. They could be quite mischievous but were generally harmless. They lived for many centuries in peace and harmony with man. Wanting to share their knowledge with future generations of humans, they wrote it down on what is known as the Emerald Tablet.

"But one day, a human race attacked them. The human race was not as advanced, nor did they have the magic the Fae possessed, but they were bigger and stronger, and eventually prevailed. The fairy folk were allowed to remain on their beloved land only if they retreated underground, into the mountains and hills. As time went by, the Fae began to be sighted. It was whispered they would come out and play amongst the flowers, in the streams, and fly through the treetops. But they remained invisible to most, for they felt they must hide from humans to survive.

"Oh, they will show themselves to you, if you

believe in them, but as more people stop believing, they are seen less and less. If the day ever arrives when everyone stopped believing in them, they would never show themselves again and would disappear forever, becoming nothing more than some forgotten legend."

Elisabeth's brows pulled in. "Do you mean they would no longer exist, or that we would never see them again?"

"One can never cease to exist. Existence is eternal. If we stop believing, then eventually, they would no longer be seen in our density, on our timeline. We cannot see what we don't believe."

"So…" Elisabeth scratched her cheek. "You believe they're real?"

"Aye, child. I do believe they're as real as you and me."

"And is the Emerald Tablet real, too?"

"The Emerald Tablet is *absolutely* real. The knowledge was written down for those wise enough to understand it. It was on display for years in ancient Egypt after Alexander the Great found it hidden in a cave. According to legend, it was later buried beneath the Great Pyramid to protect it from people who were burning libraries around the world." Bessie paused to refill Elisabeth's cup. "I'm sure it's still there today, safe. Certain men have spent centuries trying to destroy it, to suppress its information."

Elisabeth's posture perked up. "Why would anyone want to destroy it?"

"Because they want to keep the knowledge for themselves. Knowledge is power. With power, you can control people."

"Do they know what the tablet says?" Elisabeth

asked, curiosity piqued.

"Aye, it is the basis of Hermetic philosophy, and the ancient mystery schools.

Some people have spent their lifetime trying to understand its words."

Elisabeth paused to examine the woman. "Do the Fae have anything to do with my crystal?"

"Well..." Bessie stared off at nothing for a moment. "Like I said, they have had the knowledge of magic for centuries." She reached into the folds of her skirt and then held up her own shiny stone for emphasis. "Crystals are born deep within the Earth. They're living energy. The Fae learned ages ago how to harness it." Bessie paused, pointing to Elisabeth's backpack on the floor near the front door. "I'm going to guess that you have items from your time in there, right? From the future?"

Elisabeth nodded.

"Can I see some of them?"

Elisabeth took out the smartphone and Bessie gave a small yelp while she demonstrated and explained in more detail what it could do under normal circumstances.

"Now..." Bessie's eyes widened. "This item of yours...well...I can't even *begin* to understand how it works. It is absolutely amazing to me. Which makes you...much like the Fae."

Elisabeth's tummy fluttered. "I am?"

"Yes. You are from a time more advanced than my time. If you were to show your object to people here, they would think it worked as if by magic."

"Yes," Elisabeth said with a wide grin. "That's what my friends, Quinton and Fiona, said. They called them my *magic* toys."

"The same is true with the Fae," Bessie explained. "They are even more advanced than we may ever be, and they've unlocked mysteries we cannot even begin to understand. The knowledge they possess is so far out of our comprehension still. It might always be that way."

Elisabeth nodded slowly as they sat in silence at the table for several minutes. "Can *your* crystal get me back home?"

"No." Bessie shook her head. "Definitely not, child. I'm nae able to get you home with mine. But just know…you're here, in this time, for a reason, for a purpose bigger than yourself."

"Wait. What? I'm here for a reason?"

"Aye."

"What's the reason?"

"Well, we'll have to find that out now, won't we?" she said with a chuckle.

Bessie got up from the table and walked over to the hutch, removing a bowl from a lower cupboard. She placed it on the table in front of Elisabeth, and then put her crystal into it. She filled the bowl with some water from a pitcher and then sat again in her chair. She stared at the crystal for a long time.

It didn't appear to Elisabeth like anything was happening; the woman was sitting and staring at a crystal in a bowl full of water. It seemed rather…melodramatic.

After several long minutes, Bessie looked up at Elisabeth and gave her a sympathetic smile, but said nothing.

Elisabeth gasped. "What? What is it I am supposed

to do? Can you find that out in there?" She cleared her throat and looked into the bowl herself, hoping to see something.

Bessie stared again into the water. When she looked at Elisabeth, she said, "You need to restore the *honour* of Scotland."

"What?" Her brows squished together. "What does that mean? I'm supposed to restore the *honour* of an entire country?"

Bessie looked at her and shook her head. "I honestly have no idea what it means." After a long, low sigh, she said, "But, I understand when the time comes, child, *you* will know what it means."

Elisabeth's posture sagged. How was she, one insignificant little person supposed to restore honour to a country? It didn't even make sense. Her gaze darted around the cottage.

Bessie yawned, excused herself from the table, and paused in the doorway of her room. "That's enough for me tonight, child. It's very late."

"Goodnight," Elisabeth said, retying her loose ponytail with the red ribbon.

As Bessie stared at the ribbon, a thoughtful expression crossed her face and she released a deep sigh. "Good night, dear," she whispered before closing the door.

Elisabeth yawned while tiptoeing into her own room. She blew out the candle and crawled into bed, beneath dreamy, lavender-scented covers fit for royalty. Her tense muscles loosened, and she soon fell into a deep, restful sleep.

Chapter Sixteen

A crowing rooster woke her. Elisabeth lay still, listening to muffled voices outside before sitting up, rubbing sleep out of her eyes. As morning sunlight streamed through the window of her room, she climbed out of bed and stood in the doorway, yawning while glancing around the empty cottage.

She grabbed her dry clothes and shuffled back into the bedroom to dress before making the bed. A moment later, Bessie walked in the front door with a basket of fresh eggs.

"Good morning."

"Morning, lass. You hungry?"

"Almost always," she answered with a sleepy grin.

"Good." Bessie cracked several eggs into a heavy pan sitting on hot embers in the hearth. "There's bread and jam on the table already."

As they ate, Elisabeth watched people line up outside the closed gate. "Is it like this every day?"

"Pretty much," she said with a polite smile.

When they finished breakfast, Bessie walked outside, opened the wooden gate, and admitted the first person of many into her little cottage.

Elisabeth swallowed hard and averted her gaze as this one pleaded for his sores to be healed. Bessie gave her several errands throughout the day and Elisabeth did them, happy to fill the hours with something other than worrisome thoughts. She swept the cottage floor and picked vegetables from the garden, keeping busy while Bessie saw to the steady stream of visitors seeking her help and wisdom.

As Elisabeth worked, she could see Dunnottar Castle in the daylight. It was enormous, far bigger than Ealasaid. Dunnotar was a fortress perched high atop a jutting cliff; the sea surrounded it on three sides. The rock it was built on sheered straight down to the sea.

"Would you mind fetching me some seaweed, dear? I know it sounds strange, but I use it for bandages."

"Sure," she replied with a half-hearted shrug.

Bessie handed her two baskets and a knife. "Follow the footpath. You'll find your way down to the beach when you reach Dunnottar."

Elisabeth's head jerked back. "What about the army there?"

"They won't bother you. The English soldiers are mostly settled near the front gate. You're going to keep to the left at the fork before you even get to them. In any event, they're just hoping to starve the inhabitants out and won't give you a second glance."

****

After leaving Bessie's cottage, Elisabeth followed the path, winding her way toward the sea through a meadow filled with waist-high wildflowers and grasses. She gathered a bouquet of Queen Anne's lace while hiking down the steep footpath. At the fork, soldiers were assembled along the road to the right that curved upward to the entrance. The front door was set in a cleft in the rock. Elisabeth kept to the left, sprinting the remainder of the way down the trail to the beach.

The grasses ended at a rocky shoreline where seaweed-covered rocks filled the crescent-shaped bay. She turned around, looked up, and sucked in a quick breath. The castle's enormous walls of stone were set high atop the cliff. Elisabeth walked closer, staring up at the jutting rock the fortress was built on.

"Halt," an English soldier shouted, dashing down the path she'd just come from. "What are you doing, girl?"

With a gasp, Elisabeth turned, staring at him wide-eyed. "I'm just gathering seaweed, sir."

He grunted in reply before heading back up the footpath.

Elisabeth wandered along the shore, using the knife to cut strips of seaweed. When her baskets were full, she started the long trek back uphill, which left her out of breath. She lowered her head when passing the grim soldier standing watch.

After returning to the cottage, Elisabeth's posture stiffened, noticing everyone was gone except for one lone wagon.

Bessie rushed out the door, a worn leather bag clasped in her arms. "Perfect timing, lass," she said with a huge sigh of relief. "An emergency's come up and I need to tend to Mrs. Douglas. There's no need for you to come as I shouldn't be terribly long."

"All right…"

"I've sent everyone home, but if anyone comes looking for me, tell them to come back tomorrow."

She nodded, watching as Bessie climbed into the waiting carriage before being driven away.

Inside the cottage, Elisabeth filled a jug with water,

added the Queen Anne's lace she'd picked, and placed the rustic bouquet on the table. Then, grabbing a blanket, she went outside to sprawl out amongst the wildflowers, intending to lose herself in a book she'd grabbed from her backpack. She hadn't been reading long when the sound of horse hooves cantering down the dirt road disrupted her—along with the whistling of a familiar, merry tune.

Her breath caught and then warmth radiated through her body as she shoved her book under the blanket to hide it. "Malcolm!" She scaled the drystone fence, heart racing while running to greet him. "Malcolm, what are you doing here?"

He let out a huge sigh while dismounting his horse. "Do you realize…" He paused, rubbing the back of his neck. "Do you realize how much you've worried my poor sister and I?"

Elisabeth's cheeks burned and she averted her gaze.

Malcolm's voice was quiet as he slowly shook his head. "Lucky for all of us, Fiona confessed where you'd run off to."

"I'm so sorry," she mumbled. "I swear, I never meant to hurt or worry anyone…it's just…" Her chest caved in and her eyes filled with tears.

Malcolm tilted his head down, frowning. "Why'd you run away instead of returning with Fiona? I *told* you I'd protect you from that Witch Hunter, as if you were my own kin."

Elisabeth covered her face with both hands. "I didn't mean to hurt anyone, honest I didn't." Her voice quaked as she looked up at him. "Least of all you, but…"

Tammy Lowe

He swallowed hard.

"But if anyone can help me find my way home, Bessie can."

Malcolm's head flinched back slightly. "You're not *staying* here, lass," he said with a bark of laughter.

Elisabeth's fingertips reached up to touch her lips. "Yes, I need to."

Malcolm's eyes widened and then he scraped a hand over his face.

"I need to find my way home and I think Bessie may be the only one able to help."

"Old Widow Ferguson?" Malcolm cursed under his breath. "I'm of half a mind to throw you on my horse and drag you back to Ealasaid." He began pacing.

Elisabeth's chin quivered. "Malcolm, I *have* to find my way back home. To Mahone Bay…"

He let out a dejected sigh while listening.

"To my parents—"

"Look, you may not be my bairn, nor my sister's," Malcolm said with a slow, disbelieving shake of his head. "However, I do have a responsibility to protect you and know you are safe." His shoulders dropped. "If you wish to search for your parents from here, then I shall allow you to stay with Mrs. Ferguson to do so."

Elisabeth sniffled as she stared down at her empty palms.

Malcolm's brow wrinkled and he moved closer. "You always have a home at Ealasaid, lass. *Always.* You know that. If you never find your parents, our door is always open to you." He cleared his throat. "You can stay until you marry and have a home and family of your own someday."

With an uncontrollable sob, Elisabeth threw herself

172

at Malcolm, who quickly wrapped her into a bear hug. "I do know that," she said as her voice choked with tears. "And I'll never be able to thank you enough for everything you've done."

When she eventually pulled away, he turned and mounted his horse. "Oh, Shona is no longer with us, lass," he said, changing the subject.

Elisabeth's eyes widened. "You got rid of Shona?"

"Well..." Malcolm gripped the reins. "You can't have someone like that hurting the ones you love...and we've come to consider you family."

Elisabeth's chest ached, wanting more than anything to return to Ealasaid.

Malcolm took a deep breath. "Are you sure you'll not be coming back with me, lass? It would make my sister and I very—"

She closed her eyes a moment. "I wish I could, but I really need the help only Bessie can give me."

"Very well," he said with a heavy sigh. "At least we'll take some comfort knowing you're safe. I'll check on you again in a fortnight." Malcolm tipped his head. "Good day to you, lass," he said before turning his horse around, eventually disappearing down the lane.

Elisabeth trudged back to her blanket, crumpled onto the ground, wanting the pain she felt inside to end.

****

Within days, Elisabeth had settled into a routine. As Bessie tended to the sick and troubled, Elisabeth did odd chores around the cottage. When Sunday arrived, they went to the church in Kinneff. Although it was further away, an hour by horse and buggy up the coast from Dunnottar Castle, Bessie preferred it to the church in Stonehaven, and she never missed a service.

It was a quaint little kirk, seemingly in the middle of nowhere, with a small bell tower on the top. The left side of the churchyard held rows of old graves, and the entire property was enclosed with a moss-covered dry-stone fence.

They sat side-by-side on the polished wooden pew. It was the same one Bessie'd occupied year after year, listening to Reverend James Grainger give his sermon. Although Elisabeth tried to focus, her mind drifted elsewhere, easily distracted when someone coughed or a baby fussed.

Reverend Grainger was a soft-spoken, old man with a lovable face. He kept his snow-white hair brushed back, and his cheeks were so round and full she wanted to pinch them. Elisabeth could tell he was a kind and open-minded man. Bessie had told her he lived by his favorite creed: "Whatever you want men to do to you, do also to them." So Bessie, although different from everyone else, was always welcome in his church.

James Grainger, also being a man born and bred in the Scottish Highlands, was used to the superstitions he had grown up with. It was not beyond him to visit Bessie himself in search of a little medicine when he was feeling ill. Doctors were not often found in small towns and people took whatever help they could get. He would smile at Bessie while listening to her wise words, believing the good Lord, not the wee folk, had blessed her in some way when it came to helping others.

When the service was over, they filed outside with the other parishioners, passing Reverend Grainger as he greeted his flock beneath a shady tree, next to a cracked headstone. The man smiled at Elisabeth, and then turned to Bessie. "You have a wee visitor this morning."

"Aye, Reverend." Bessie had a gleam in her eye. "This lovely lass is my kin. She's staying for a while."

"Lovely to meet you, my dear," he said in a warm tone. "I hope we meet again during your stay." Turning to Bessie, he said, "I never realized you had any living relations."

"Aye..." She winked at Elisabeth. "The lass is a distant relation on her father's side."

After a few minutes of small talk, Bessie said farewell to the minister.

While heading home, the clip-clop sound of the horse's hooves trotting along the narrow road almost lulled Elisabeth to sleep. The path then darkened as they drove beneath a canopy of leaves ablaze in autumn colors. When a speeding carriage slowed as it pulled up behind them, Elisabeth glanced over her shoulder at the driver. Her eyes widened, watching as pompous-looking Robert Hobson, with his big gray sideburns and his nose pointing straight in the air, overtook them at a wider section in the road. She let out a huge breath when he continued on.

****

"I'm glad we came to Stonehaven for market day, lass." Bessie flashed a strained smile. "I have a feeling you're far more homesick than you're letting on."

Elisabeth smoothed down her dress. "I'm fine."

"Well..." Bessie shrugged her shoulders. "The distraction might do you some good."

Elisabeth twisted her wrists as they walked through the town. The market was filled with merchants selling wool and pottery, leather hides, oatmeal, butter, and cheese. Entire herds of goats and sheep had been brought in. Rows of tables held fresh produce, and people haggled over prices as small children ran through the market square.

Someone gasped. "Elisabeth? Elisabeth!"

She held her breath at the familiar voice and turned around in time to see Fiona running toward her with outstretched arms.

They both squealed, grabbing each other into a big hug.

"I've been worried sick about you." Fiona let out a shaky laugh. "I begged my father to bring me here just to see if I might find you. If you didnae show up, I was planning on faking some terrible illness and telling him I'd only survive with help from Old Widow Ferguson. Are you all right? I heard you found her."

Elisabeth's hands trembled. "Oh my gosh, Fee...I'm still here, but I'm fine. And I did find Old Widow Ferguson, this is her," she said, gesturing to Bessie beside her.

Fiona's mouth fell open. "You don't look at all like an old—"

"You must be Fiona." Bessie grinned. "I've heard an awful lot about you." Then, turning to Elisabeth, she pointed across the street. "I'm going to sit in that pub for a wee bit. You two visit a while and I'll wait for you in there."

Elisabeth bit down on a smile. "You don't mind?"

"Not at all, lass."

With wide grins, the girls linked arms and strolled through the Mercat Square.

"You have to see the bonnie ribbons over here,"

Fiona said as they tried to muscle their way through the packed market to the other side. The shouting around them made it impossible to hear each other.

The crowd began chanting.

Elisabeth's brow wrinkled as she listened closer, trying to make out the words.

It seemed Fiona heard it at the same time.

"Burn the witch! Burn the witch!"

The girls looked at each other wide-eyed before standing on tippy-toes, trying to see over the heads of the crowd. There, set up beside the mercat cross, was a simple wooden gallows. A noose swayed from it, awaiting someone's neck.

One man's voice was louder than everyone else.

Standing on the raised platform of the gallows, Robert Hobson had an old woman by the arm. He shouted back at the people, praising them for bringing forth the witch.

"Thou shalt not suffer a witch to live!"

The excited crowd roared their approval.

"Burn the witch. Burn the witch!"

Elisabeth shook uncontrollably, but couldn't look away, feeling as if she was glued to the spot.

"That's him!" Fiona shouted into Elisabeth's ear so her friend could hear her. "That's the same man who came to arrest you, isn't it?"

A hand to her mouth, Elisabeth nodded, watching as Robert Hobson slipped the noose around the woman's tiny neck.

At that moment, a young man grabbed Elisabeth by the arm and turned her around to face him. "Elisabeth?" He grabbed her other arm and stared down at her, saying nothing for a moment as his eyes filled with tears. "You're…" His voice quaked. "I can't believe…" An uncontrollable sob escaped.

Elisabeth's posture relaxed and her eyes narrowed, trying to place him. He looked to be about nineteen years old, yet his tormented blue eyes seemed ageless. With a slight shake of her head, she tried to step back, but he held her with a firm grip.

He then winced and let go. "Oh, God, I'm sorry. I'm so sorry. You must think me mad. I didn't mean to startle you."

"It's fine," she replied in an uncertain tone.

"Elisabeth, you don't want to see this," he said, referring to the execution about to take place. "Bessie waits for you. Go."

Elisabeth rubbed her eyebrow as she continued to stare at the stranger, taking in his shoulder-length golden brown hair and stubbled beard. He wore brown pants, not a kilt, and his gray shirt peeked from behind a tattered beige jacket that was nothing more than rags. How did he know her name? Had she met him at Bessie's cottage? So many people were in and out all day long. He looked so distraught that part of her wanted to reach out and hug him.

"You look familiar."

He jerked his head back and then opened his mouth to say something, but no words came out.

Elisabeth's own eyes prickled with tears. Her tummy fluttered, like there was more—some sort of connection. She didn't know him from Bessie's cottage, but darned if she could remember where they might have met.

Fiona suddenly grabbed Elisabeth's hand and pulled her out of the square, in the direction of the pub where Bessie was waiting.

When Elisabeth glanced behind to look at the stranger, their eyes locked. He looked like she felt, like he carried the weight of the world on his shoulders. The two continued to stare at each other as Fiona led Elisabeth away, eventually disappearing around a corner.

Fiona's mouth fell open. "Who on earth was that?" A huge grin then spread across her face.

"I…" Elisabeth's brow furrowed. "I honestly have *no* idea. Maybe I saw him at Bessie's?"

Her head jerked back. "Oh…well…I'd have sworn you two knew each other." She bit her lip. "He's right, though. If the witch-hunter is here, you should definitely go."

Elisabeth cleared her throat. "I thought they burn witches at the stake?" she said, thinking about the old woman's fate again.

"Aye, they hang 'em first. They burn them after so the devil can't re-enter their body."

Her heart raced; thankful she managed to escape from Hobson when he came for her at Ealasaid.

They met up with Bessie at the pub, and when it was time to head to their respective homes, Fiona and Elisabeth said their goodbyes.

"I don't know when I'm going to see you again. I'll come to market with my father as often as possible, so I can see you. You come to market days often, too… if you are still *here*."

Elisabeth hugged Fiona goodbye, all the while holding back tears.

"I hope you find your way home again," Fiona whispered in her ear.

****

Elisabeth tilted her head to the side. "Do you know how time travel works?" she asked over breakfast the next morning.

"Not at all, lass," Bessie said with a chuckle. "I should be asking *you* how it works."

Elisabeth let out a heavy sigh. "I was hoping that…" She stopped, staring at Bessie with a dazed look after being interrupted by loud noises outside of the cottage. She ran to the door, watching an army advance past them, toward Dunnottar Castle. Her mouth fell open. "You gotta see this."

Bessie's eyebrows rose as she crossed the room.

Standing in the doorway, they both watched the procession. The townsfolk, waiting to see Old Widow Ferguson, stood watching the unfolding scene, as well. Row after row of soldiers marched past, many on horseback. Elisabeth looked in the direction they were coming from. A long line of men carried and pushed all manner of equipment: cannons and muskets, catapults and trebuchets, amongst other weapons.

"I fear it's only a matter of time before Dunnottar falls." Bessie clutched both arms to her chest. "I don't want you collecting seaweed from the shores by Dunnottar anymore, lass. I should have enough to use as bandages for a while."

Elisabeth's brow wrinkled while nodding. "Yeah, I'm not really into hanging out in war zones anyhow."

When the procession finally ended, they turned back into the cottage, attempting to resume their daily routine.

Later that morning, someone banged on Bessie's front door.

Elisabeth's brow furrowed. Nobody ever knocked. Everyone just waited politely next to the stone fence.

Although Bessie's posture perked up while opening the door, Elisabeth's body tensed when she saw it was Robert Hobson, along with two other men.

He puffed out his chest. "Bessie Ferguson?"

"Aye..." she paused to examine him. "What can I do for you?"

Suddenly, one of his men grabbed Bessie, pulling both arms behind her back.

Elisabeth gasped

"I am Robert Hobson, the Witch-Finder General, as appointed by Parliament." He flashed a cocky grin while walking with his wooden cane into the cottage. "And you are under arrest on charges of witchcraft."

The color drained from Bessie's face. "This is all a mis—"

"What is your name, child?" Hobson asked, turning his attention to Elisabeth.

"Leave her out of this." Bessie's nostrils flared. "She's naught but a wee lass."

Elisabeth backed away in quick jerky steps. When smashing into the table, it suddenly occurred to her that although the witch-hunter knew her name—he didn't know what she looked like. Her breath burst in and out as her mind raced.

"Your *name*, child," Hobson repeated with a scowl as he banged his cane on the stone floor.

Before she could decide if it was a good idea, or a terrible one, Elisabeth's shoulders tightened and the lie tumbled out of her mouth.

"Anne Shirley." She lowered her voice to a whisper. "My name is Anne Shirley, sir."

Her hands trembled. It was the first name that popped into her head.

Anne of Green Gables.

At least the infamous book hadn't been written yet.

Hobson wrinkled his nose while staring at her then turned to one of his men. "Arrest her young apprentice, Miss Shirley, as well."

"No!" Bessie yelled. "Leave her alone. The bairn has *nothing* to do with me." She shook her head in denial. "I'm *begging* you to leave her alone. I'm just minding her for a friend…"

Elisabeth squeezed her eyes shut. One way or another, Robert Hobson, the witch-hunter, was going to catch up with her, either as Elisabeth London, or now as Anne Shirley.

Chapter Seventeen

Sarah's heart raced when Henry, now a grown man, burst through the front door.

"Grandma, there's been an accident," he said with an emotion-choked voice. "Quick! Where are the medical supplies?"

Gasping for air, Sarah bolted from her chair and hurried to the cupboard to grab what she could find. "Oh, dear God. What made all that noise? Is Granddad all right?"

This treasure hunt had turned into one calamity after another. Even the cofferdam ended in failure, when a storm came through and destroyed it all. The Truro Company, too, had exhausted their funds. The excavated hole was now being called the Money Pit.

"There's been an explosion." Henry's hands shook while grabbing the rags and ointments from Sarah. "Stay here."

Sarah ignored him, lips and chin trembling as she followed her grandson to the pit. She arrived out of breath, looking all around. "John?" she screamed in a shrill voice. "John!"

Men were running around barking orders, adding to the mass confusion.

Her chest caved in, watching a group of people huddled together.

A wave of cold washed over when she craned her neck in time to see a pair of unmoving legs.

"He's gone…" Anthony said with a disbelieving voice.

Sarah let out a primal scream, running toward the crowd of men.

"Grandma, no!" Henry yelled as he turned around, but she pushed her way through.

She froze, staring at the remains of a man lying on the ground.

He was so mangled she couldn't tell—

"Sarah! Sarah!"

Her head jerked back.

John's voice choked with tears as he grabbed Sarah's arm, pulling her away from the dead body. "I'm here. I'm fine."

"John?" She covered her mouth with her hand. "I thought it was you. I thought it was you." She fell against him, shaking all over. "Oh God, I thought it was you."

He hugged her tight, until she stopped trembling.

John's chest caved in. "It's the Prescott boy. It happened so fast. We've had no luck damming the water in Smith's Cove away from the beach, so they've been working on another shaft. They hit another one of those darned flood tunnels and were using a steam pump. But, the boiler exploded. It just exploded." John's voice choked with tears. "Oh, God, Sarah, he was just a boy, not even twenty. How can we tell his parents he's dead?"

In silence, John held Sarah in his arms for a long time.

The Money Pit had just claimed its first victim.

****

The tolbooth was an old stone building, rectangular in shape, set amongst houses and shops clustered near the harbor. From the street, Robert Hobson pulled open a heavy wooden door, and Elisabeth and Bessie were dragged inside by his men.

Sun streamed through a barred window in the otherwise dark jail. In the distance, Elisabeth heard the jingle of iron, probably from handcuffs or leg irons. Prisoners muttered to themselves as footsteps paced back and forth.

As they were hauled across the stone floor to a metal door, the guard's shoulders pushed back while fiddling with his set of keys.

Elisabeth's breath came in short gasps. The smell of sweat and mildew overwhelmed her.

"You know, 'twas once a storage building for Dunnottar," the guard said to the witch-hunter. "Now it's Stonehaven's jail and court."

"Aye." Hobson's eyes narrowed when Elisabeth stared up at him. "The perfect place to try thieves, murderers, and *witches*."

The iron door swung open and she was shoved into the crowded cell. When it slammed shut, Elisabeth grabbed the cold, hard bars in both hands.

"Can you feel the stench of *hopelessness* in the air?" a man muttered, followed by a maniacal giggle.

Bessie grabbed Elisabeth's arm, leading her to the far end of the cell. There, they sat on the floor in silence.

"I know you," whispered a woman crouched in the corner. "Yer Miss Bessie. You saved me son last summer." She pressed her fingers to a toothless grin.

"Thank you."

Bessie nodded, forcing a watery smile into place. "Why…why are *you* here?"

"She stole shix…shix…half a dozen sheep," a man with a greasy receding hairline answered. "From the McLaughlin farm" He paused to let out a long belch. "And is gonna hang tomorrow for it."

The woman lowered her head, picking dirt off her skirt. "Aye, tis true."

"Are ye here on charges of witchcraft?" the man asked Bessie too loudly.

"Aye," she replied.

"And yer…" He waved his arms at Elisabeth in slow motion. "Yer lass, too?"

"Aye."

His posture relaxed. "I thought as much. I'm here 'cause they say I's being a public nuisance and need to sober up." He rolled his eyes.

"I can't imagine," Elisabeth whispered.

The man lurched forward. "Want me to tell you what's gonna happen to you's two?"

"Not particularly," Bessie warned in a sharp tone.

He sagged against the wall. "Oh." Then his eyes widened. "Ohhhh, you dinnae want me scaring the lass."

Bessie nodded tightly, as if holding back an insult.

"In that case, I'll jis tell you what happened to Mary Campbell, instead."

Bessie gasped. "Mary Campbell? I know Mary."

"Aye, well, Mary was arrested and brought here, to the tolbooth." He paused, blinking rapidly as if trying to focus on Bessie. "There's an old man here this morning. Brought in, you know, to sober up too. He

186

told me all about what they done to Mary, for he saw much of it with his own two eyes.

"First thing the witch-pricker done was he brought Mary outside and threw the hag into the sea. He declared to all present if she floated she was a witch. Said water is a symbol of the church and if she floats that means it dinnae accept her. Well, Mary floated to the top. After that, Hobson brought her to another room and tied her to a chair. Wouldn't let her sleep or eat for some thirty hours. If she did begin to fall asleep, one of his men would hold her up or drag her 'cross the floor to keep her awake. Then he took his big pin and pricked her all over, looking to see if it hurt her."

He paused, and then whispered, "Just 'tween you and me, I even heard his pin is retractable." The drunk sucked in a quick breath. "The old man said her clothes were stripped off her and the witch-hunter looked all over for devil marks. When she couldnae take it anymore, he brought her back here to rest up, and then would drag her out the next day to start it all over again. Kept it up till she confessed, he did. The next morning came and she still said she weren't a witch." The drunk finally lowered his voice. "He said Mary 'ventually confessed when Hobson brought out the thumbscrews 'cause, I guess, she couldnae take the pain any longer."

Bessie's chest caved in. "What's become of Mary?"

"She dies on the morrow, with the sheep thief." He then pointed to a fabric-covered lump on the floor. "Mary's right there."

Bessie gasped, then rushed to the spot he had pointed to and lifted the blanket. Elisabeth helped Bessie roll Mary onto her side so she could cradle the woman in her arms, all the while stroking the matted hair, pushing it from her face. Mary Campbell looked no older than Elisabeth's own mother.

"I'm sorry…" Mary took a deep, pained breath and closed her eyes. "They…they made me say your name, Bessie." Her arms fell to her side, lifeless. "Just say you're guilty…confess to get it over with. Either way, they win."

An eerie quietness spilled over the room as Bessie rocked Mary.

Elisabeth's pulse raced, and she squeezed her eyes shut, wondering when the witch-testing would begin. Was Mary right? Would it be better to lie and say she was a witch to save herself the brutal torture before hanging? Elisabeth shook her head in denial. Feeling lightheaded, she rocked back and forth.

Elisabeth must have nodded off at some point because she awoke with a start when the door to the cell swung open. Two large men marched into the room, grabbing hold of Mary Campbell and the sheep thief, the two women who were sentenced to die today.

Bessie sniffled, wiping at her nose after Mary was ripped from her arms.

"I'm sorry…I dinnae mean it," was all Mary could say as she was dragged out of the room.

Elisabeth moved closer, rubbing Bessie's back.

"Dinnae worry, it'll be over quick for them both," the drunk said, trying to sound comforting.

****

The next morning, the metal door swung open again.

"Bessie Ferguson and Anne Shirley."

A wave of dizziness washed over Elisabeth and she

noticed Bessie's chin tremble.

"Come with me," the guard ordered.

With a slow walk, Elisabeth followed as they left the crowded jail cell and climbed a wooden staircase.

Holding back tears, she began to shake uncontrollably when the man reached for the door handle.

What torture devices awaited them in the room on the other side?

When the door opened, Elisabeth's brows squished together as they were brought straight into what appeared to be the courtroom.

Bessie walked in, head held high.

So many people were present that there was standing room only, with spectators flowing out the door. Angry faces filled the court, but the angriest looking of all were Robert Hobson and Reverend Grainger who stood in the middle of the room.

Elisabeth's shoulders curled forward while looking at them both. It was hard to tell which man was more furious, the witch-hunter or the minister.

Reverend Grainger's fists clenched and unclenched. He let out a guttural roar when he saw Bessie and Elisabeth walk into the courtroom and take a seat on a wooden bench. He then turned to Hobson, spittle building up in the corners of his mouth. "I've no idea how it's done elsewhere, but you're in Stonehaven now." His nostrils flared. "I assure you Mrs. Ferguson is most certainly *not* a witch. This matter should never have been brought before the town council. We *forbid* you to do more of your witch-tests on these innocents. You're supposed to have permission from the crown, written permission, to extract a confession through means of torture. You have none. Nor did you have any for poor Mary Campbell, God rest her soul."

Hobson forced a laugh. "Reverend Grainger, most towns welcome me with open arms. You are doing Stonehaven a great injustice. I am here, appointed by Parliament, to seek out witches."

"You've no evidence against Bessie Ferguson, nor the girl," Grainger said, glaring at the witch-hunter.

Hobson let out a quick, disgusted snort. "Actually…Mary Campbell identified Mrs. Ferguson as a witch. You need only to open your eyes and glance around you to see all the people here eager to testify against her today."

The reverend took a step back. "Aye, Mary Campbell confessed because you'd nae stop torturing her until she named names!"

Hobson put on a smile. "I will let the good people of this town decide whether or not this witch and her apprentice are to burn. I am the Witch-Finder General, and as I said, I have been appointed by Parliament. I am merely doing my duty, sir."

"Well, then let me be the first to testify in defense of Bessie Ferguson. She is nae a witch. Nor is the lass. Good day, sir." Reverend Grainger stormed to the back of the courtroom, where he leaned against the wall, arms crossed.

"Order! Order!" The judge tried to control the overflowing courtroom as a buzz of excitement rose.

"Please rise, Mrs. Ferguson."

Bessie stood, hands trembling while her gaze drifted across the packed courtroom.

Robert Hobson stepped forward, his nose wrinkling as he stared at Bessie. "Mrs. Ferguson, you are a healer, are you not?"

"Aye, I am a healer."

"You are here today to answer the charges brought against you of witchcraft. Do you plead guilty or not guilty?"

"Not guilty."

"You may call your first witness, Mr. Hobson," the judge said.

As Bessie and Elisabeth sat on a wooden bench in the crowded courtroom, one by one, everyone filed past the witch-hunter, waiting in line to testify. The color drained from Bessie's face and she lowered her head. How could they all betray her like this? Elisabeth gripped a wooden railing in front of her, waiting for all the people to turn on Bessie.

But something amazing happened instead.

"Bessie's nae a witch," a woman snapped. "She saved me whole family."

A man waved his hand in dismissal. "Aye, I'll say nothing bad about Mrs. Bessie. She's no witch. The bairn's done nothing, either. I've only seen her doing chores and helping fetch seaweed and the like. You've got no witches here today, mister."

"How can she be a witch, sir? All she ever done is charity, acts of kindness, and healing folks. No, she's done nothing but good works. How can that be evil?"

One at a time, all the people Bessie had helped over the years stood up for her, said their piece, and then walked out of the building, Reverend Grainger leaving with the last of them.

The courtroom was empty of anyone to testify against her.

The judge shot the witch-hunter a dismissive

glance. "Do you actually have anyone to testify against this woman, Mr. Hobson, or are you planning on wasting any more of my time?"

"Um, uh…" Hobson touched his throat while stammering.

"I cannot try a witch if there is no evidence, Mr. Hobson," the judge said in the deserted courtroom. "Bessie Ferguson, you are hereby acquitted of the charges of witchcraft brought against you. You are free to go."

Bessie swallowed and nodded. "Thank you, but I'm not leaving without the lass."

Mr. Hobson stepped toward Elisabeth, who was glad he still had no idea of her true identity. He did have accusations against Elisabeth London, and someone willing to testify against her. But here, today, she was Anne Shirley and she had only been arrested because of her association with Bessie.

"Miss Shirley, you are also here today to answer the charges brought against you of witchcraft. Do you plead guilty or not guilty?"

She kept her face blank. "Not guilty."

The judge glanced around the empty courtroom. "I'm guessing you have no witnesses for the child either, Mr. Hobson?"

He bowed his head. "It appears not."

"Miss Shirley, you are free to go as well. There doesn't seem to be any sort of evidence against you." The judge then glared at the witch-hunter. "Mr. Hobson, in the future would you be so kind as to not waste the court's time? We have no interest in becoming part of your witch frenzy here in Stonehaven, and I have serious doubts as to the legitimacy of your claims of being appointed by Parliament. Good day," he said as he stood and left the courtroom.

Chapter Eighteen

The first thing Bessie and Elisabeth did when they returned home was eat. They'd had little more than a drop of water and a crust of bread while locked up and were famished. In silence, both shifted in their seats, listening to the raging battle in the distance. The sounds of screaming men, of cannons and muskets, carried across the fields, filling the air with ominous cries. Dunnottar Castle was going to fall, sooner rather than later. The time had come.

When finished eating, Bessie's shoulders pushed back and she grabbed her shawl from a hook. "I'll be back shortly."

Elisabeth flinched. "Where are you going?"

"You wait here. I have to hurry. My husband is gravely injured."

Elisabeth's eyes bulged. "Wait...what? Your *husband*?" she asked, following Bessie out the door as she started running across the field heading toward Dunnottar Castle. "What do you mean your husband?" she yelled. "I thought you were a widow?"

"I am. I need to get to him as quickly as possible."

"Well...I'm coming with you!"

Bessie stopped and spun around. "No. You're to stay here. Do you hear me?"

Elisabeth frowned.

"It's far too dangerous. I'll be back as quick as I can," she said before running toward the battlefield.

Elisabeth paced back and forth, listening to cannonballs battering the walls of the fortress as the battle cries continued. Metal on metal slashed and an explosion rocked her seconds before flames lit up the sky. She took deep breaths to calm herself, watching the horizon, willing Bessie to come back.

After what seemed an eternity, Bessie appeared in the distance. Supporting a tall, wounded man, his arm was thrown around her neck as she half dragged him to the cottage.

Elisabeth let out a sigh of relief and ran toward her. "What can I do?" she asked with a shaky voice.

Bessie's husband's head was bent over, hair covering his face. The semi-conscious man was drenched in blood.

"Get the door!"

Elisabeth ran, clearing the way. Bessie was a strong woman and managed to get him inside and flop the wounded man onto her bed.

"Fetch some water from the well…and gather all the rags you can find. I need to wash and dress his wounds."

With a curt nod, Elisabeth grabbed a bucket, running to the well behind the house as fast as possible. When returning, she searched for clean rags. "I think I've got everything." Rushing into Bessie's room, Elisabeth peered at the man's face for the first time as he moaned in pain. Her posture then stiffened, and she let out a sharp yelp.

She was staring at Malcolm.

Elisabeth ran to the bed, shaking her head in denial.

"Malcolm?" He was covered in so much blood she was hard put to recognize him. "Malcolm? Oh my God….don't die. Please don't die…" she muttered over and over again as her voice choked with tears.

"Elisabeth?" He squirmed in discomfort while reaching for her hand. "Elisabeth."

A wave of cold washed over her. "What were you doing there? At Dunnottar?"

"Our…plan…it didnae work." His back arched and he slipped in and out of consciousness.

Elisabeth grabbed a rag, helping Bessie wash the blood off him. Her eyes then narrowed. "Malcolm is your husband?"

"Aye," she said with a crisp nod. "Well, he will be. He doesn't know it yet."

Elisabeth gave her a dazed look. "What?"

"Pass me another rag…"

Malcolm, seeming to have regained consciousness, grabbed Bessie's arm. "I'm not your husband."

"Not yet you're not," Bessie said with a flushed appearance. "I'll agree to fix you up, if you agree to marriage. Just so you know, you're in pretty rough shape and not likely to live without my help. But, it's up to you."

Malcolm gave her a dazed look. Despite his injuries, he tried to chuckle, but started coughing and closed his eyes again. "Are you mad, woman? I cannot marry you. I dinnae even know you."

"Elisabeth, hand me some seaweed, dear. I need it to bandage him up. He's losing a lot of blood."

Malcolm struggled as he reached into the leather sporran on his belt and took out a yellow piece of fabric, clutching it in his fist. "I've failed," he whispered with a trembling chin.

Elisabeth's brows squished together. "What are you talking about? How have you failed?"

"I was…supposed…to get the Honours."

Her head flinched back slightly. "What?"

"They're at Dunnottar, by the sea." Malcolm paused, clenching his teeth. "The garrison inside is watching for my signal." He opened his hand to expose the bright yellow cloth. "I was attacked before I could get there."

"I don't understand," Elisabeth said with a slight shake of her head. "What are you supposed to do?"

"I was trying to save the Honours of Scotland."

Elisabeth gasped.

"Reverend Grainger in Kinneff is waiting to hide them. He's prepared a spot."

Her eyes bulged as she looked at Bessie. "The Honours of Scotland? Bessie, this must be what I'm supposed to do. I've got to go." She then looked down. "How can I leave Malcolm like this, though?"

Bessie covered her mouth with a hand. "Restoring the Honours of Scotland is your way home, child. I told you you'd know what to do when the time came. Malcolm will be fine with me." She cleared her throat. "Go. Find your way back home, lass."

Malcolm shook his head. "No…Elisabeth. Not you…it's too dangerous. In Stonehaven…find Hamish Rose. He's—"

"No…" She felt the color drain from her face, realizing she'd be heading straight into the battle. "I have to try."

He grimaced in pain before slipping into unconsciousness again.

Elisabeth pulled the yellow cloth from his hand and headed for the door.

"The Honours of Scotland have been at Dunnottar the entire time?" Bessie said with a disbelieving voice. "Och! The answer was right before me all along. That's what the garrison has been protecting all these months." Bessie's voice was shaky. "Wait, take the baskets, child."

"Why?"

"To hide the Honours in," she said, grabbing two large baskets.

Not waiting for a clearer explanation, Elisabeth stuffed Malcolm's cloth into the waistband of her apron, grabbed the baskets, and ran out the door toward the path.

Bessie's voice was faint in her ears. "Be careful, Elisabeth."

With rasping breaths, Elisabeth stood at the top of the cliff, looking down at the battlefield. The garrison of men defending Dunnottar Castle fired at their attackers below. With a pounding heart, Elisabeth ran down the footpath, dodging flaming projectiles flung at the English. At the fork, Cromwell's heavy cannons struggled to pound the castle walls high above them. Meanwhile, soldiers with a battering ram attempted to break down the main door. All around her, men fought hand-to-hand.

Elisabeth's shoulders tightened as she made her way beyond the front line, shaking uncontrollably while trying to reach the shoreline. She heard the drawn-out hisses of arrows flying through the air. With wobbly legs, she sprinted down the steep trail, away from the heavy fighting. Her heartbeat raced, nearly exploding as she made her way along the path through waist-high weeds and grasses, straight to the beach beneath the cliffs. Once there, she bit her lip while staring up at the castle, perched high atop its stone mountain.

In the distance, a man was leaning far out of a window.

Elisabeth trekked over the rocks, along the coast, slowly making her way closer. She waved, trying to get his attention.

When he held his hands up, as if asking a question, her eyes narrowed in confusion.

The yellow fabric!

Elisabeth grabbed the yellow cloth, waving the bright fabric in the air so the man could see the signal.

His head disappeared. Seconds later, he was back, lowering a large burlap sack tied to a long rope. The bag inched closer and closer, slowly sliding down the moss and rocks of the cliff-side. Elisabeth shook out her hands while eyeing the beach and footpath, watching for soldiers. She could still hear the battle taking place as Cromwell's men tried to storm the only entrance. When she reached the sack, the man released the rope and disappeared again. With an empty feeling in the pit of her stomach, Elisabeth loosed the rope and ran to hide behind a huge rock.

Once hidden from any soldiers who might be close, she opened the bag. Her eyes bulged and mouth fell open. Inside was a magnificent, solid gold crown surrounded by red velvet and fur, covered in gemstones and pearls. She became still realizing it would take all day to count the jewels.

Setting the crown aside, she reached into the sack again; removing a silver scepter topped with a pearl and a gigantic crystal ten times the size of Elisabeth's.

The third item was a sword whose hilt was graced with oak leaves and angels. Almost as tall as she was, it was tucked into a wooden scabbard covered in silver and red velvet with silk and gold embroidery.

Foamy waves crashed against the rocks where she hid, holding priceless treasures. She squeezed her eyes shut, wondering how to smuggle the very treasure they were fighting for, through the front lines of the ongoing battle, and all the way to Reverend Grainger in Kinneff.

Elisabeth's head jerked back when she saw two soldiers running down the steep path. She ducked behind the rock, frozen in place while spying on them.

The men looked up and down the beach as if searching for something. Elisabeth then let out a huge sigh of relief when they turned, heading back up toward the main entrance of the castle. With a fluttery feeling in her chest, she started back to work, quickly wrapping the crown in the sack and tucking it into one of the baskets she'd brought. She then placed the scepter in the other basket. While grabbing handfuls of seaweed to cover the treasures with, her hands shook so much it seemed to take twice as long.

Elisabeth took a deep breath, trying to calm herself. The sword was too big to hide. She brought a shaky hand to her forehead.

Think, Elisabeth, think.

Suddenly, she remembered how other women carried heavy baskets by using a long wooden pole across their back, hanging the baskets on both ends. Could she disguise the sword in the scabbard as a piece of wood? She laid the sword down and started wrapping seaweed around it. Layer after layer, as if applying bandages. It wouldn't be perfect, but might buy her some time.

Moments later, she paused, glancing all around. The sounds of battle overhead had stopped, replaced with cheers and shouts. Elisabeth rubbed her eyebrow then took the seaweed-covered sword and balanced the baskets on either end of it, the crown tucked in one and the scepter hidden in the other. She took a deep breath, kneeling in front of the sword, praying it looked like nothing more than a piece of driftwood. She then stood, balancing it on both shoulders, behind her neck.

Elisabeth bit her lip, making her way over the rocks to the shore, and then heading up the steep pathway, praying the soldiers she'd seen earlier had rejoined the others. Her pulse raced while peering at each end of the scabbard, making sure the seaweed still covered the baskets filled with treasures.

Just before reaching the fork in the road, she let out a quiet exhale, noticing the main battle itself had moved. The castle entrance had been breached.

"Halt! What is your business here?"

Elisabeth froze. She looked up at two soldiers rushing down toward the beach. "I'm just gathering seaweed—"

"It's fine. Just a servant girl I see 'ere almost every day." He then turned to Elisabeth, shaking his head. "You got a death-wish, kid? Get outta 'ere 'fore you get yourself killed."

"Hey! Norris, Lovell..." A third soldier yelled from the path leading to the castle. "The garrison finally surrendered. Come on...we're being sent inside to search now."

The soldiers hooted in excitement and dashed off.

Elisabeth watched as the men rushed toward the main gate. She then started up the steep hill, arriving out of breath once reaching the top of the cliff. Then, instead of taking the path toward Bessie's cottage, she followed the narrow road that led to Kinneff.

Riding in Bessie's horse and buggy on Sunday, it had taken about an hour to reach. She guessed one could walk there in a little over two hours.

With a grave expression, Elisabeth stared back at the damaged walls of the castle. Smoke billowed from parts of it. Dunnottar now looked like a wounded soldier itself. Wind feathered through the grasses as she followed the dirt road. The sounds of war eventually replaced with the whirring of grasshoppers. Her posture then stiffened, realizing the soldiers were, at that exact moment, searching high and low for the treasure she carried. A wide smile surfaced. Who'd ever believe she had been so brave? A heroine. Her. Wasn't she the pathetic one who couldn't even hit a baseball in under eighteen attempts? Wasn't she the one who caught fly balls with her eye? The one who still couldn't mount a horse without sufficient help? She didn't know how, but this was her ticket home and worth any risk. She'd done it. She couldn't wait to tell Malcolm.

Malcolm.

Her brow wrinkled.

Oh, please, God, don't let him die.

Elisabeth marched as fast as she could. A little over two hours later, she reached the door of the church.

Reverend Grainger's head flinched back after opening it. "Can I help you, child?" he asked while glancing around the yard, clearly searching for someone else.

"I hope so. I have something I think I'm supposed to bring to you?"

His posture went rigid. "You? What's become of Laird Craig?" he whispered.

Elisabeth cleared her throat. "He's...he's been badly injured so I have the... *honours.*"

Reverend Grainger's shoulders dropped at the news of Malcolm. "Quick, come inside, lass." He grabbed her baskets while peering around once more to see if anyone was coming. Once inside, he locked the doors.

With a slight moan, Elisabeth set the sword and baskets down. After rubbing her neck, she bent and pushed the seaweed aside, lifting out the scepter.

"Oh, my word..." Reverend Grainger said with a slow, disbelieving shake of his head.

Next, Elisabeth lifted the sack from the other basket and pulled the crown out.

Reverend Grainger stood, speechless, as she handed him the wooden scabbard.

"Here's the sword. I'm sorry it's all muddy and dirty. I tried my best to disguise it."

Reverend Grainger raised his eyebrows. "You, my dear, have single-handedly restored the Honours of Scotland."

"What *exactly* are the Honours of Scotland? I mean, I've got these treasures, but—"

He held his arms out wide, as if hugging the world. "Why, the Honours are these, the crown jewels of Scotland."

Elisabeth squeezed her eyes shut. "Wait...what? The crown jewels? *The* crown jewels?"

The old priest burst into laughter. "Aye, they are

indeed the crown jewels of Scotland, lass, and you've saved them from a terrible man named Oliver Cromwell. He is trying to destroy them. He's already destroyed the British crown jewels."

Her voice rose in pitch. "Why?"

"Well, after King Charles was executed, Cromwell considered the British crown jewels to be...*unnecessary* and managed to get his greedy hands on them. He then sold the jewels to the highest bidder and melted down the gold." Grainger shook his head. "Cromwell's naught more than a barbaric plunderer if you ask me, and we Scots couldn't let him get these." A wide grin spread across his face. "You did it, my dear girl. You saved them."

Elisabeth clutched her belly and leaned in. "Do you by any chance have a crystal necklace that belongs to me?" She'd done what she was supposed to do. That much was clear. She wanted to go home now.

"A crystal necklace?" he asked in an uncertain tone. "No, child, I cannae say I have."

A sudden coldness rocked Elisabeth to the core.

"But if I find it, I will personally deliver it to you," he said in a soothing tone. "I, nae, all Scots, are forever in your debt."

Elisabeth's chest caved in, shoulders slumped.

Reverend Grainger's brow furrowed as he looked toward the door. "Soldiers are everywhere. We need to hide the Honours quickly, lass. I've been preparing what I hope is the perfect spot."

He walked toward the altar and lifted a large stone that sat in front of it, revealing a hollow large enough to hold the treasure. Elisabeth placed the crown, the sword, and the scepter into the large cloth sack and handed it to the reverend.

"Oh, no, I wouldn't dream of it. Will you do the *honour*?" Reverend Grainger said.

Lips pressed together, Elisabeth nodded and knelt to place the items into the hole, but something seemed to be in the way. "They won't fit," she said with a slight shake of her head. "There's already something in here."

"That's impossible. I dug that hole myself."

Elisabeth put the sack beside her on the ground and reached an arm into the hiding spot to grab the obstruction.

"What on earth...?" Reverend Grainger tilted his head to the side. "Who put that there?"

Elisabeth sucked in a quick breath, pulling out a beautiful box that looked like it belonged with the rest of the crown jewels. Made of polished wood, it was encrusted with pearls and gemstones. Her mouth fell open, staring at the name engraved on the lid.

Elisabeth.

She took a deep breath and slowly opened it.

Her head fell back and tears welled behind her eyelids. There, on velvet lining, sat her crystal necklace.

"Is...is that what you were looking for? I have no idea how it—?"

"It doesn't matter now," Elisabeth said with a huge grin while fastening it around her neck. She then put the box aside, grabbed the Honours of Scotland, and lowered them into the hiding place.

Reverend Grainger replaced the large stone into the floor. Then, they stood back, satisfied smiles on both their faces. Everything in the church looked normal, just as it had before opening the secret place.

Elisabeth could now return home. She felt for the

familiar crystal pendant as it lay below her throat. Warmth radiated through her body. She couldn't leave without saying goodbye, though, and she had to ensure Malcolm was okay before returning to her time.

"I have to go." She waved goodbye to Reverend Grainger and started for the door, planning to run the entire way back to the cottage.

"Wait, lass. I'll get my carriage and take you to Bessie's. I insist."

"That would be wonderful," Elisabeth said, filled with emotional gratitude. "Thank you."

"Don't forget this exquisite box."

Elisabeth sucked in a quick breath while holding it in her hands. "It's quite something, isn't it?"

Chapter Nineteen

As Reverend Grainger drove to Bessie's house, Elisabeth sat silent in the buggy, tracing a finger along her engraved name on the jeweled box. Embedded with rubies, sapphires, and emeralds, her brows squished together, trying to figure out *why* it was given to her. The fact that the uncommon spelling of her name was used, with an "s" and not a "z", suggested it was left by someone who knew her well.

When they turned down the lane leading to Bessie's thatched-roof cottage, Elisabeth looked up, noticing the setting sun had painted the sky a dramatic orange. She took a deep, satisfied breath, listening to the clip-clop sound of the horse hooves while traveling the dirt road one final time.

Other than a fancy carriage parked out front, there was no line of people waiting along the stone fence, seeking help from Old Widow Ferguson. The moment they came to a stop, Elisabeth jumped from the buggy and sprinted to the door.

Bessie ran outside. Visibly shaken but happy, she wrapped her arms around a beaming Elisabeth. "Oh, thank God, you're back. I've been worried sick about you." She then lowered her voice to a whisper. "Well...?"

"I did it. The honours are safe and I have my

crystal."

Bessie's posture slumped in relief. "You have some guests inside." With a wide grin, she took hold of Elisabeth's box for her. "Go see."

Elisabeth stepped into the white-washed cottage and both hands flew to her chest. Quinton sat at the table, eating biscuits while Fiona paced back and forth. "How's Malcolm?" she asked when Lady McQuade appeared in the doorway of Bessie's bedroom.

His sister's eyes went up, heavenward. "Fortunately, the stubborn man is going to be just fine."

"Oh, thank God." Elisabeth reached out to Fiona, pulling her into a hug. "Look…" She held her crystal necklace out for the room to see. "I did it. I found it. Now I can go home again."

Lady McQuade let out a huge breath. "Thank goodness."

Fiona's posture slumped. "We thought you were dead." She wiped her nose with the back of her hand. "We heard Old Widow Ferguson and a girl were arrested for witchcraft. I just *knew* it was you and we tried to get to Stonehaven as quickly as possible."

Quinton shook his head in disbelief. "When we got to Stonehaven this afternoon, the courtroom was empty and we were told it was all over. We thought for sure it was too late. We thought you were, well, you know—"

"Aye…" Fiona's voice choked with tears. "We thought you'd been hanged."

Elisabeth squeezed Fiona's hand. "I'm fine. Everything is *perfect* now."

"Curious thing…" Lady M's posture perked up. "While returning to Ealasaid, completely devastated I might add, we happened upon a young man Fiona recognized."

"Aye, it's the one we saw in the Mercat Square." Her eyes widened. "Remember him?"

"Yes!" Elisabeth sucked in a quick breath. "How could I forget?"

"Well, *he* stopped the carriage." Fiona leaned in. "Told us to turn around because we'd find the two of you, alive and well, at Bessie Ferguson's cottage. Then, he pointed us in the right direction before walking away." Her gaze went distant. "It's like he somehow knew that—"

"Elisabeth…?" A quiet voice coming from the bedroom interrupted.

Her brow wrinkled and she dashed to Malcolm's side. "Are—?" Both hands covered her mouth as she stared at him. "How do you look so much better already?" The blood had been washed from his body, and he had been bandaged by an expert, but he no longer looked to be at death's door. "What the heck is in Bessie's water?"

"Aye, I feel much improved." He exhaled while looking up. "My future wife is nagging me to death already, though." When Elisabeth offered him a bemused smile, he pulled her closer, whispering in her ear. "This Bessie…she's a bonnie lass, isn't she?" He chuckled.

Bessie heard him as she walked over to the bedside. "Aye, and when you're better I want a proper proposal out of you. I'll not be telling our children of such an unromantic betrothal." A crooked grin spread across her face. "Now stop talking and take another drink of the healing water."

"Ugh…are you trying to drown me, woman?"

Malcolm wiped at his mouth in an attempt not to laugh. "You've spilled it all over me."

"Well, stop talking and moving around so much, you old fool," Bessie said while wiping the spilled water off his brow with a dry cloth.

Elisabeth's mouth snapped shut as she stared at the two of them. There was definitely a spark.

"Good thing I'm here today, isn't it?" Reverend Grainger announced from the doorway. "I hear I have a wedding to perform?"

"Not so fast, Reverend!" Malcolm turned, giving Bessie a wide-eyed look that caused everyone to burst into laughter.

When Bessie and Lady McQuade began to fuss over Malcolm again, Elisabeth whispered to Fiona, "Are you all right? I mean, about you know who?"

"Aye. I'm fine." She let out a sigh. "My first broken heart, that's all. He was too old for me, anyhow," she added with a smirk, before glancing at Quinton.

He grinned back at her.

"Well…" Lady M cleared her throat. "Regrettably, it's time to take our leave. Quinton, have the driver ready the horses please, darling."

"All right, Mother."

The woman kissed her brother on the cheek, before looking up at Bessie. "You'll take good care of him?"

"Of course."

"I will call again in a few days. He's…he's going to be all right, isn't he?"

Bessie squeezed Lady M's hand. "Dinnae you fret. He's going to be just fine," she said in a soothing voice.

Lady McQuade took a deep, satisfied breath and

then turned to Elisabeth. "Come along, my dear. I must say, I'm glad you're returning home now. It hasn't been the same since you left."

Elisabeth's chin quivered, realizing the woman's mistake. She grabbed her backpack while following Lady M outside. It was time to say goodbye. Elisabeth loved these people like family, but she didn't belong here. Although it had been a grand adventure, she never wanted to risk losing her parents, ever again. That was too much for her heart to handle.

"Actually...I'm going *home* home. To Mahone Bay." She gave a hard obvious swallow behind Lady McQuade, who froze rather than stepping into the carriage. "And I will never be able to thank you enough for everything you've done for me."

Lady McQuade turned around to face her, lips pressed together into a slight grimace.

Elisabeth's voice choked with tears. "I am going to miss you so much, but I'm finally going *home*."

"Oh..." The woman's shoulders dropped, and then she hitched them back up again. "My mistake, I assumed—" She gasped when Elisabeth squeezed her eyes shut and pulled her into a tight hug. When she finally let go, Lady M distracted herself by digging through a small drawstring purse. "I...um...I have something for you, dear. The timing is quite fortuitous really because, at long last, I have finished it." She pulled out a dainty white handkerchief. "It's not much, but I made it for you."

Elisabeth's lips parted, holding the needlepoint she'd frequently seen Lady McQuade working on. It had the most intricate scalloped edges, embroidered forget-me-nots, and dot accents. In the center, stitched in beautiful curly letters, were her initials, EL.

"Every young lady needs a handkerchief."

Elisabeth teared up. "Thank you so much. I…I had no idea—"

"Remember…" She clasped both Elisabeth's hands in her own. "Our door will always remain open to you," she whispered before climbing into the carriage.

Quinton cleared his throat. "I'm not fond of goodbyes," he said before following his mother into the carriage.

Elisabeth grabbed his arm. "Wait!" She reached into her backpack for the comic book she'd put in there so long ago. "This is yours. I actually bought it *for* you." With a smile, she handed him the colorful book.

His eyes widened. "Really?"

"Really. You keep it and maybe think of me when you read it."

A huge goofy grin spread across his face. "Thanks!"

"You don't have to thank me. We've already seen the movie," she said with a smirk. "You've been a wonderful friend, Quinton, and I'll never forget you." She gave him an awkward hug and stepped back.

He nodded, staring down at the futuristic book that was his to keep, and then climbed into the carriage.

From inside, Lady McQuade looked down at the glossy pages and yelped. "What on earth…?"

Quinton burst into laughter when he looked up and saw her bewildered expression. "Mother, Fiona and I are going to have to tell you all about where Elisabeth is from on the way home."

Fiona sniffled, arms hung limp at her sides.

Elisabeth took a deep breath, gulping at the air.

"Fee, I'm going to miss you like crazy. You're the best friend I've ever had, and I'll never find anyone like you." Her chin trembled. "You're…you're such a great person."

Tears streamed down Fiona's cheeks.

"Wait here. I have something for you." She ran back inside, grabbing the jewel-encrusted box that her crystal had been in, and raced back to Fiona. "I want you to have this."

Lady McQuade and Quinton both gasped from inside the carriage when they saw the item.

Fiona's head jerked back. "Elisabeth! No! This is, this is…I cannae take this."

Elisabeth's shoulders pushed back. "Yes, take it, Fee. This will change your life, your family's life." She spoke in a steady, low-pitched voice. "You can have beautiful clothes and hire a tutor and learn to read. Just think of all the books you could buy. Your little brother and sister can go to school and be whatever they want to be when they grow up. I don't need these jewels, Fiona, like you do. I already have all these opportunities."

"No, Elisabeth, it's too much. I cannae accept it…"

"I insist. You are taking it." Elisabeth pushed the jewel-encrusted box into Fiona's hands and hugged her goodbye as tight as she could. "You can be a real princess now with your very own library full of books."

Quinton whooped loudly while hanging out of the carriage. "Are you mad? Take it, Fee, before she changes her mind!" His mother yanked him back down into his seat.

Fiona softly shook her head while staring at the letters engraved on the box. "What does it say on the top?"

"*That* is how you spell my name. Elisabeth with an S, kinda like Anne with an E."

"Elisabeth…with an S." Her nose wrinkled. "Your name will be the first word I learn how to write." Still sniffling, Fiona climbed into the carriage.

The horses pulled away down the lane and Elisabeth ran after them, waving goodbye while her eyes clouded with tears. She chased the carriage until they were far ahead of her and she was out of breath. They were gone now, forever. Elisabeth swiped away tears and started back toward the cottage.

That was when she saw him.

He was sitting beneath a tree, his horse grazing nearby. Had he been there all along?

A slow smile built as she marched closer. "You? Who are you?" she asked the man in the tattered jacket. "You know me, don't you?"

He hesitated a moment and then stood, walking toward her with slow, languid movements, the horse's reins held loosely in one hand.

She moved toward him, repeating her question. "You know me, don't you?"

The young man let out a huge sigh. "Like the back of my hand, Elisabeth. I know you like the back of my hand."

Her heart started to race. "But, I don't know *you*."

"Yet," he answered. "Yet."

Her lips parted as she stared at him. Although no older than nineteen or twenty, his eyes still appeared ageless. There was something…inexplicable, almost magical about him. In a way, he reminded her of the man she had met years ago who taught her how to catch the fireflies. He said he had powers that were like magic. And he had even known her name. Elisabeth's hand covered her mouth. "Wait a minute...are you a...?"

"A time traveler?" he suggested.

"Yeah. Is *that* how you know me?"

"No." With a small shake of his head, he looked away. "It's more...*complicated* than that. "We'll meet in the future. You save my life, you know."

"Really?"

"I see you got your crystal back," he said quietly, changing the subject. "That's good."

"You put it there for me to find, didn't you?"

He nodded. "I took it from Shona—"

Elisabeth's head flinched back slightly, "Wait...was that you I saw riding away from Castle Ealasaid just before Robert Hobson arrived to arrest me?"

He wiped at his mouth, holding back a smile. "I was there that day, yes, to get your crystal back for you."

She let out a spontaneous laugh. "How?"

"A sleight of hand trick you could say. But, I left it where I knew you'd find it."

"Why didn't you just give it back to me?"

"It's a long story. One you'll learn over time. I don't want to change the course of events. Not *yet*. For now, all you need to know is I left the quartz crystal there, in your box, for you to find."

"My box?"

His blue eyes then widened. "Wait...you just gave it to Fiona, didn't you?"

"Yes, I..."

The man shook his head, trying not to laugh. "Of course you did." His posture relaxed and he stared at her for a long moment, saying nothing. "Well..." He then looked away to mount his horse.

Elisabeth noticed his eyes had filled with tears.

From atop his steed, the man seemed to have regained his composure. "Until we meet again," he said with a nod and a playful grin, before riding away.

Elisabeth froze, completely spellbound while watching his horse trot down the road.

"I'm going to be leaving as well, my dear, before it gets too dark," Reverend Grainger said as his buggy pulled up beside her.

"Oh!" Her eyes widened. "I didn't even hear you coming," she added with a small laugh. "Goodbye, Reverend. It has been wonderful knowing you."

"The pleasure has been all mine, my dear. You are a special young lady and have done a remarkable thing." He clucked to the horses, the buggy jerked, and then continued down the road.

When Elisabeth neared the stone fence, Bessie walked out of the cottage. The sun was ready to begin its descent in the sky.

"I want to tell you something before you leave, lass."

Elisabeth's posture perked up. "Yes?"

"In about three months, I'm going to become pregnant."

Her brows squished together. "How do you know *that*?"

"Well, I have it on good authority, from a certain young man, that Malcolm and I will be wed and parents within a year." Her gaze then darted toward the tree the man had been sitting under.

Elisabeth suddenly became still. "Really?"

"I thought you might like to know the bairn is going to be named after her great-granddaughter, well, actually her fourteenth time great-granddaughter."

"I think you mean great grandmother," Elisabeth said. "She can't be named after her great-granddaughter."

"No, I spoke correctly. She's going to be named 'Elisabeth,' after her great-great-great-great...well, you get the idea. Fourteen times."

"Huh?"

Bessie stared at her and smiled.

Elisabeth's eyes then widened. "Are you my...?"

"Aye. I'm your fifteenth-time great-grandmother."

Elisabeth stood speechless.

"You heard correctly, lass," Bessie said with a bark of laughter. "Like I told Reverend Grainger, you *are* my kin on your father's side."

Elisabeth took a slow step back. "That means Malcolm is my—"

"Aye, he's your old grandfather," she said with a belly laugh. "Well, fifteen generations from you of course."

Elisabeth pressed both palms to her cheeks.

Bessie shrugged her shoulders and let out a satisfied sigh. "It's true." She then glanced at the road. "I see you were talking to David."

"David?" Elisabeth's eyes inexplicably prickled with tears. "You...you know him?"

"Aye, he's the one who gave me my crystal when I was just a wee lass after I took a fancy to it. Mine is just glass, you know," she said with a wink. "But, David's the one who put the magic in my well. It's *his* water that heals the people. I've known him almost my entire life. For as long as I can remember, he would visit and check in on me."

Elisabeth moved in closer, hanging on to every word. "He said he's not a time traveler. Is he...is he one of the fae you talked about?"

Bessie burst into laughter. "Oh Lord, child, no. David was an acquaintance of my father." Her voice then choked with emotion. "And he looks exactly the same as the very first day I met him when I was just a wee bairn."

Elisabeth's eyes narrowed. "How is that possible? He doesn't look that old."

"Elisabeth...David is immortal."

Her mouth fell open. "Immortal? What do you mean immortal?" She stared down the road to see if she could see David, but he was long gone. "Bessie...what do you mean by that? I thought he said..."

Bessie didn't answer. Instead, she turned and headed toward the cottage door.

Elisabeth let out a long, low sigh while looking around one last time. The setting sun sent sparkles across the fields of wildflowers as she breathed in the salty sea air. Sensing a kind of magic in the air, she broke into a run, heading straight to Malcolm's bedside.

Elisabeth reached out, grasping his hand. "I'm going to miss you...Grandpa." She then wrapped her arms around his neck and planted a big kiss on his forehead.

"Grandpa?" he asked with a silly grin on his face.

"Or...do you prefer Grand*father*?" Elisabeth asked with a chuckle.

Malcolm's brows squished together in confusion as he held her hand in his. "I've *no* idea what you're talking about, lass," he said with a snort.

Her smile then wavered. She didn't want to leave him yet. Her heart began to physically ache and she turned away. "I'm going home," she whispered.

"Home?" A slow smile spread across his face. "That's good. You belong at Ealasaid."

She took a deep breath. "Home to my parents. To Mahone Bay."

"Oh." He let out a dejected sigh. "Well, that's good news, right? Aye, I suppose that's where you *truly* belong."

"Definitely." Elisabeth gulped at the air.

Malcolm looked at her. "You...you were like the daughter I never had," he whispered.

Her chin trembled as she tried desperately not to cry. "I saved the Honours. They are safe and hidden now. I did it."

His mouth fell open. "You did?"

"Yes. I did. I did it. They're safe."

"Thank you, lass," was all he said as he closed his eyes while still holding her hand in his. "Thank you."

"I'd do anything for you," she whispered, wiping a stray tear away. Within moments, he was sleeping again. He was going to be okay though. He was going to live. "Goodbye, Malcolm." She pulled her hand from his. "Goodbye, *Grandpa*."

"Bessie..." Elisabeth said with a satisfied sigh as she wrapped her arms around her. "I'm finally going home."

The woman stroked Elisabeth's hair and adjusted the red bow that tied it back. "Go, child, and God speed."

Elisabeth stepped away, pulled the backpack over her shoulder, and then closed her eyes while twirling the crystal in her fingers.

Thoughts of home on her mind.

Home.

Chapter Twenty

John sat in his rocking chair, nodding off while staring into the fire. He was an old man now, near the end of his days.

"Mr. Smith, I'm on my way out," a soft voice said to him. "I left dinner for you on the table and I'll take your laundry home with me. Is there anything else I can do for you before I leave?"

"No, thank you, Jane. That's everything," he replied without looking up.

"Also, there's a man here to see you. Says his name is David. David Perrier?"

John's brow wrinkled, but then his mouth fell open and he straightened up in the chair. "David Perrier? As I live and breathe." He chuckled. "Send him in, send him in."

With hesitant steps, David entered the room. "Hello, John."

John struggled to rise from his rocking chair, a huge smile on his face. "I haven't seen you in at least sixty years—" He then froze, staring at him.

"Sit down, my friend, sit down. Don't get up for me."

John's head flinched back "Oh, I…I apologize. I thought you were…you must be David's grandson? Great-grandson?" He let out a nervous laugh. "I have to say, you are the spitting image of him," he reasoned while lowering himself back into the rocking chair.

"No, John, it's me."

He shook his head while openly staring. "No. That's *not* possible. David Perrier would be close to ninety years old."

David sat in a chair opposite his friend and let out a shallow sigh. "Well, that's not *impossible.*"

John's posture stiffened. "Am I dead? Are you the angel of death?"

"You're very much alive still." He gave him a pained look. "Although I worry I might cause you unwarranted stress."

John couldn't take his eyes off David's. He stared into them for a long time, searching for an answer. His hand then covered his mouth. "It is you, isn't it? How?"

"How is Sarah?" David asked, changing the subject.

"Oh, my dear Sarah." John reclined back in his rocking chair and his shoulders drooped. "She's been gone these last few years. I miss her something terrible." His eyes filled with tears and both men remained silent a few minutes, lost in their own thoughts. "Why did you come back?" he asked quietly.

David gave a half-hearted shrug. "I came back to Nova Scotia. I'm building a house not far from here. I'll stay for a few years, until I have to leave again."

John let out a deep sigh. "That's why you left, isn't it? You didn't want us to see you don't age. How? This is not possible."

"It's hard." David looked down, studying his hands. "I hate this."

"Why are you here now? I mean, with me?"

"I'm here because of the treasure."

John's head jerked back. "We still haven't got it out. I pray every single night I'll know what's down there before my dying day, but—"

"You've had the treasure for years, John. I was there when you got it. I've seen it myself in your house."

His breath hitched. "Are you mad? We've never gotten anything out of there."

"Think."

John's brows squished together, but then his gaze drifted to the fireplace, resting on the green colored stone he'd mounted for Sarah into the mantle all those years ago. He glanced back at David.

David nodded.

"That's nothing," John said while rubbing an eyebrow. "That's just a—"

"*That* is everything." He sat quietly, fidgeting with a small rock he pulled from his pocket. "That's the most sought-after treasure in the history of mankind."

John's eyes widened. "It's just a stone."

"It's not just a stone. I've kept that safe for a very long time."

"How long?"

David laughed, but his eyes didn't. "Too long."

"Wait, how is that possible? How could you keep it safe?" He fell silent and then a thought, too wild to be true, occurred to him. He looked at his friend. "Did *you* build the pit?"

David's head was bent, but he lifted his eyes to John, who could see the answer in them.

"You?"

"Well, I had some help. It was a very long time

ago."

John's voice rose in pitch. "What the hell kind of stone is that?"

David took a deep breath. "It's known by many names. The Philosopher's Stone, The Emerald Tablet, The Holy Grail, The Chintamani Stone…"

John sank further into his chair. His heart started to beat faster and he was sweating. "Those are all different treasures."

David shook his head. "They are one and the same." His brow wrinkled when he glanced up at John. "Are you all right? You're not looking very…" He scrubbed a hand over his face. "I'm sorry. Perhaps I shouldn't have come."

"No, I'm fine. I want to know this." John's voice was soft, full of wonder. "Perhaps excitement like this isn't very good at my age, but I need to know. I have spent a lifetime trying to learn what was down there."

David replied with a small nod. "Do you know what they say about the Holy Grail?"

"No," John said while rubbing his left arm.

"They say if a man doesn't understand its power, it would simply disappear before his eyes."

"It's been right in front of me for sixty years. Invisible." They both sat for a few moments without saying a word. "I thought the Grail was a cup?"

David shook his head again. "There are as many grails as there are grail stories. The first mention of it being a cup was in a twelfth-century poem, based on an even older Celtic myth. The author died before he finished it, and many people wrote many different endings. But that," he said, pointing to the fireplace, "is the very thing all the legends are based on. It's amazing how stories grow and change over time. It was a cauldron in some stories, a stone in others."

"You said Emerald Tablet. That stone's not an emerald," John pointed out.

"Originally, emerald only meant green stone. Any kind of green stone." David

reached into his bag. "May I?" he asked, pulling out a hammer and chisel.

John shrugged his shoulders and let out a small laugh. "I wouldn't be able to stop you anyhow, would I?"

"Thank you." David chipped away at the fireplace to remove the tablet.

"It's the words, isn't it? What do they say?"

"They're ancient Sumerian. Only thirteen lines, but when translated and studied and understood, it is an information guide to the entire universe and how it works. It's full of hidden meaning, a formula, if you will. The knowledge it contains is so powerful, some men have tried to suppress it since the dawn of time and keep the knowledge to themselves. It's been in the hands of Alexander the Great, King Herod, Titus, Apollonius of Tyana, Nicolas Flamel..." He opened his mouth to say something, but stopped, rubbing a hand against his heart instead.

With a slow, disbelieving shake of his head, John stared into the fire.

"It was given to mankind so it could be shared, but the world and men to which it was given has changed."

John tilted his head to the side. "Who gave it to mankind?"

David shrugged his shoulders and then pointed toward the sky. "The world is not ready for this information anymore," he said as he removed the stone and slipped it into his bag.

"The Philosopher's Stone? Isn't that for changing metals into gold, and it's the…" John's eyes widened as he stared at David. "The elixir of life." He gasped. "*That's* why you don't age."

David nodded and sat back down. "The *curse* of my life. It turns base metal into gold, yes, but it's much more than that."

"The Holy Grail is the Philosopher's Stone is the Emerald Tablet?" John murmured, beginning to understand the scale of what David was telling him. "Why? Why did you let it be found then? Why didn't you put it at the bottom of the pit?"

"It was perfectly hidden for hundreds of years. If someone stumbled across the hiding place someday, it was hidden in plain sight. You were all so busy trying to get to the bottom of the pit you didn't think anything of the stone. I saw it in your house and had to laugh."

"Is there anything else down there?" John asked. "Seems you can make the elixir of life; I'm assuming you can make gold?"

David raised his eyebrows but his eyes gave nothing away, except a sadness deep inside him.

"Why here? Why on earth Oak Island?"

"Because I wanted to watch over it. And I wanted to be here. Near her."

"Who?"

"Nobody." His voice became tearful. "I should go now."

"No, please…old friend," John said in a soothing tone. "Who?"

David's chest caved in. He reached into his shirt

and pulled out a small leather sack tied to a string around his neck. His fingers trembled as he opened it up. Inside, was a tiny painting of a smiling woman whose long hair was as dark as her big brown eyes. She looked to be about nineteen years old.

"Well, she is certainly lovely. Who is she?"

"Elisabeth," David whispered, almost to himself. "*Cor meum*. My heart."

John gave an understanding nod. "Why aren't you growing old with her? That was your advice to me all those years ago. You told me to buy land and grow old with Sarah."

David looked up and let the torment in his eyes say it all.

"Oh...I see." John stared down at the floor, recognizing the pain. "I'm so sorry."

"I wait for the day when...when I can undo tragic events and make everything right again." He paused, chin trembling. "But the waiting is agony." As David replaced the portrait in the tiny sack and tucked it away, his brows furrowed. "I live a thousand lifetimes to grow old with her once." His voice cracked and he turned, holding back a sob. "I wouldn't wish this *hell* on anyone."

"Oh, dear God, David..." John's voice choked with tears as he pulled himself out of the rocking chair. "What kind of life have you known?"

David's shoulders slumped as he walked over, drawing him into a warm hug. "Goodbye, my friend."

John grasped the handles of the chair to steady himself as he stood speechless.

David made his way to the house he had spent the last few months working on. He had poured his heart and soul into every detail. One last thing remained. He unwrapped the stone that was in his bag and ran his fingers over the symbols, recalling all the joy and pain it had brought him. He then applied mortar to the back and inserted it into the foundation where he had left a spot for the cornerstone. It was hidden once again, and would remain there for several more centuries. David then stood back, holding his breath while admiring his work. The house was perfect. Exactly as Elisabeth had described it.

Chapter Twenty-One

It didn't matter that it was a perfect autumn day. The kind where the air is so crisp, the trees so colorful, even teachers will do just about anything not to have to spend it indoors. With a lightness in her chest, thirteen-year-old Elisabeth London couldn't stop grinning. She finally had gym class outside last period. She didn't hate gym class. Actually, she kind of liked it now.

With wide steps, she walked up to home plate.

Everyone was yelling.

"You can do it, Elisabeth!"

"Remember, you can't strike out," her gym teacher, Mr. Keddy, said. "You can try as many times as necessary to hit the ball."

She nodded, knowing his dumb rule didn't help anyone. It was humiliating. Practice with Quinton is what made the difference.

"Remember to keep your *eye* on the ball," Will teased.

Elisabeth gave him a half-hearted shrug, planted her legs in a wide stance, and lifted the bat up into position.

Hands up, elbows out, step forward, swing while it's in front...

"Okay, might as well look for a spot to nap now. Wake me up when she actually hits the ball, guys," Will said as he lay down on the grass.

Mr. Keddy frowned. "William, get up."

Will stood and let out a melodramatic moan. "Let's get ready for strike one."

Elisabeth took easy breaths, waiting for the pitcher to pitch.

"Anyone want to place any bets?" William continued. "Five bucks says it takes her over twenty attempts today? Anyone? Anyone?"

The pitcher finally pitched.

Elisabeth's brow furrowed while whacking the ball as hard as possible.

She then jumped up and down before running to first base.

Her classmates went wild as the ball sailed through the air.

"Go! Go! Go!" they shouted to her.

She sprinted to second base.

"I've got it!" William shouted, holding his glove up over his head.

"RUN!" they kept shouting as Elisabeth raced to third base.

Suddenly, the class started roaring with laughter and she glanced behind to see what the commotion was. Confused, she came to a sudden stop.

William fell to his knees.

Holding his private parts, he grunted in pain as his eyes watered.

"What happened?" she asked with a bark of laughter.

"Karma," her friend Emma said with a snort. "Instant karma."

****

The leaves crunched underfoot as Elisabeth walked home from the job her dad set up with one of his patients. Every day, on her way home from school, she'd stop and make tea and sandwiches for Mrs. Waters, a sweet, but lonely and slightly eccentric old lady who lived nearby. In exchange for a light meal and companionship, the old woman paid a healthy allowance.

While shuffling down the quiet street, Elisabeth rubbed the back of her neck, thinking about the crystal. It sat on her dresser, untouched since her return. She certainly missed everyone, but a sinking feeling always crept into the pit of her stomach.

What if she went back and something went wrong again?

Elisabeth belonged here, in the twenty-first century, with her parents.

She'd kept all the clothing, along with the delicate hanky Lady McQuade had made for her, in a box hidden at the back of her closet. Elisabeth let out a shallow sigh, knowing they were all she had to remember her Scottish friends by.

When reaching home, her posture perked up. Something caught her eye, shining behind a row of sunflowers lining the driveway. Elisabeth crept closer and then gave a small yelp. There sat her box: the box she found in the church in Kinneff, the box she had given to Fiona, the box that had her name engraved on it, the box David said was hers.

Her lips parted as she picked it up, looking at it in her hands. She then held her breath and glanced all around. If David had put it there, he was nowhere to be found.

Staring back at the box, she saw an empty spot where one of the gemstones used to sit. All the rest were still there. With a slow, disbelieving shake of her head, she noticed the box looked older, as if she hadn't seen it for three hundred years. It looked like a well-worn and loved antique. A wide smile spread across her face as she lifted the lid. Inside was an envelope, yellow with age. Her heart raced as she broke the seal, unfolded it, and began to read.

Dearest Elisabeth,

I am writing this letter and praying it finds its way to you, as promised. You will be so proud to learn that I can now read and write. The box you gave me changed my life and the life of my entire family. One single diamond was able to let my father buy land and educate Ellen, Ian, and myself. We are forever in your debt.

It has been ten long years since we last saw you. Know you are missed and remembered every day here at Ealasaid. You may be surprised to learn Quinton and I were married three years ago and we are expecting our second child in two months time. We have a two-year-old daughter named Anne. I am sure you can guess the inspiration of the name. Lady Margaret is the most doting and loving grandmother that ever lived.

As for Malcolm and Bessie, they have been happily married for many years now and their daughter, Elisabeth, is almost nine. They adore her to bits.

I don't know if you remember David Perrier. He is the mysterious man we encountered so many years ago in Stonehaven. He came to the door of Ealasaid last evening, apparently an old acquaintance of Bessie's. I recognized him immediately as he doesn't look to have aged in all these years! (I am envious.) He asked if I still had your box and looked so happy when I told him yes. He asked me if I would allow him to return it to you someday as he would find you in the future. Bessie assured me he would. I was shocked when he presented a bag full of gold as compensation for it. He doesn't look like one to have a single shilling, let alone an entire bag of gold! I told him I have all the riches I need, because of you. I only want to return this box with sincere thanks.

I am writing this letter on this, the 15th day of February 1662. I pray you read it someday. God Bless you, Elisabeth. You are much loved.

Your faithful friend,
Fiona McQuade

Chapter Twenty-Two

John sat on the front porch of his beloved house, a frail old man oblivious to the fading red paint as he rocked back and forth. Here on Oak Island, men still continued to dig the Money Pit. Instead of watching the excavations, he would stare across the island, often wondering about David Perrier. His posture relaxed, knowing he'd take their conversation with him to the grave. He could leave this world content now, finally knowing the secret buried deep in Acadia.

He'd spent his entire life searching for treasure, when the real thing was in front of him the entire time—in more ways than one. John Smith leaned back and took a deep, satisfying final breath. He was going home, to be with his Sarah once again.

The End
of the tale of John Smith.
But take heart,
For as you probably guessed, Elisabeth's adventure is
far from over.
To be continued...
Book Two: The Sleeping Giant

Author's Note

The digging at Canada's Oak Island continues to this day and throughout the years has attracted treasure hunters such as John Wayne and Franklin Roosevelt, before he became president of the United States. It has claimed six lives, the first when an exploding boiler killed an unknown worker. In 1897, Maynard Kaiser fell to his death, and in 1967, the Money Pit claimed four lives in one day: Bob and Bobbie Restall, Karl Grasser, and Cyril Hiltz.

In the nineteenth century, it was claimed the missing stone had been deciphered to read: Forty Feet Below, Two Million Pounds Are Buried. This translation is thought by many to be a hoax used by those who were seeking financial support in the dig. The inscribed stone found in the pit, and later mounted into John Smith's fireplace, disappeared without a trace. No rubbings or copies of it were ever made.

The legends of how the Honours of Scotland were smuggled out of Dunnottar Castle remain shrouded in mystery. They only tell of a young servant girl smuggling them to safety, on the pretense of gathering seaweed. Reverend Grainger kept the secret buried deep beneath the floor of his little church for close to a decade. They still remain the oldest set of crown jewels in the British Isles, and the second oldest in the whole of Europe.

A word about the author...

An adventurer at heart, Tammy has explored ruins in Rome, Pompeii, and Istanbul (Constantinople) with historians and archaeologists.

She's slept in the tower of a 15th century castle in Scotland, climbed down the cramped tunnels of Egyptian pyramids, sailed on a tiny raft down the Yulong River in rural China, dined at a Bedouin camp in the Arabian Desert, and escaped from head-hunters in the South Pacific.

I suppose one could say her own childhood wish of time traveling adventures came true...in a roundabout way.

http://www.tammylowe.com